FEB 2010

DATE DUE

APR 2 1 2010		OCT 0 8 2012	
		JAN 1 7 2013	
JAN 3 0 2011		APR 0 8 2014	
FEB 1 0 2012		APR 0 3 2015	
FEB 2 3 2012			
APR 1 6 2012			

NASCAR HEROES PRESENTS

FROM ZERO TO HERO

JEREMY DIAMOND
writer

MATT CASSAN
PETER HABJAN
artists

KENNY HUTMAN
JAMIE CRITTENBERGER
executive editors

JONAS DIAMOND
editor

STARBRIDGE MEDIA GROUP, INC.
publisher

JOHN GALLAGHER
series editor-in-chief

Spotlight

NASCAR
LIBRARY COLLECTION

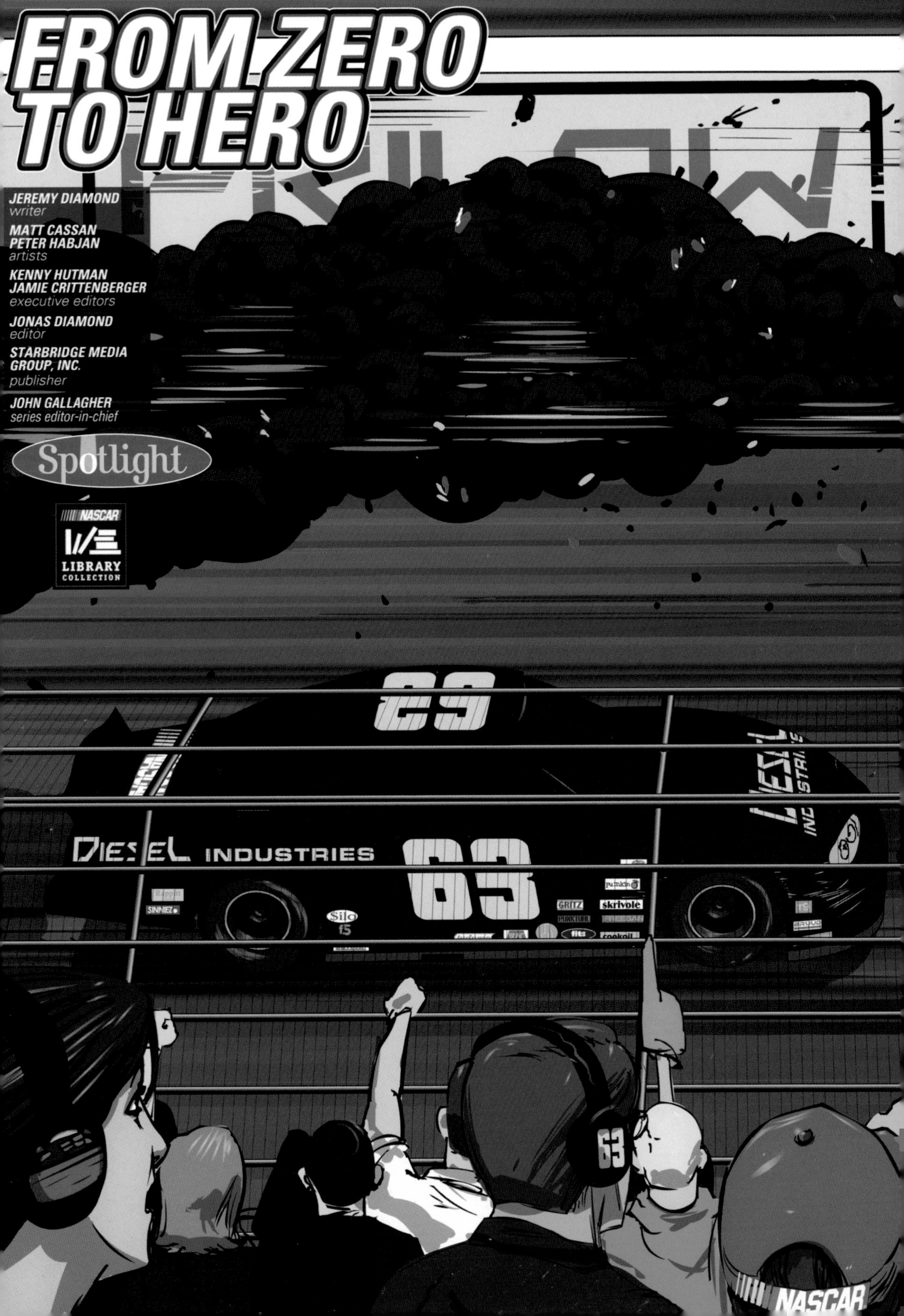
63
DIESEL INDUSTRIES
63
skrivole
NASCAR

VISIT US AT
www.abdopublishing.com

Reinforced library bound edition published in 2010 by Spotlight, a division of the ABDO Group, 8000 West 78th Street, Edina, Minnesota 55439. Spotlight produces high-quality reinforced library bound editions for schools and libraries. Published by agreement with Starbridge Media Group, Inc.

Library of Congress Cataloging-in-Publication Data

Diamond, Jeremy.
  From zero to hero / Jeremy Diamond, writer ; Matt Cassan and Peter Habjan, artists. -- Reinforced library bound ed.
      p. cm. -- (NASCAR heroes ; #1)
  "Nascar Library Collection."
  Summary: When Dashiell James, janitor for Jack Diesel's racing team, causes an explosion in a secret laboratory, he becomes Jimmy Dash, lead driver for Team Flatstock, known on the circuit as "Team Laughingstock."
  ISBN 978-1-59961-662-9
  1. Graphic novels. [1. Graphic novels. 2. Automobile racing--Fiction. 3. NASCAR (Association)--Fiction. 4. Science fiction.] I. Cassan, Matt, ill. II. Habjan, Peter, ill. III. Title.
  PZ7.7.D52Fro 2009
  741.5'973--dc22

                              2009009007

All Spotlight books have reinforced library bindings and
are manufactured in the United States of

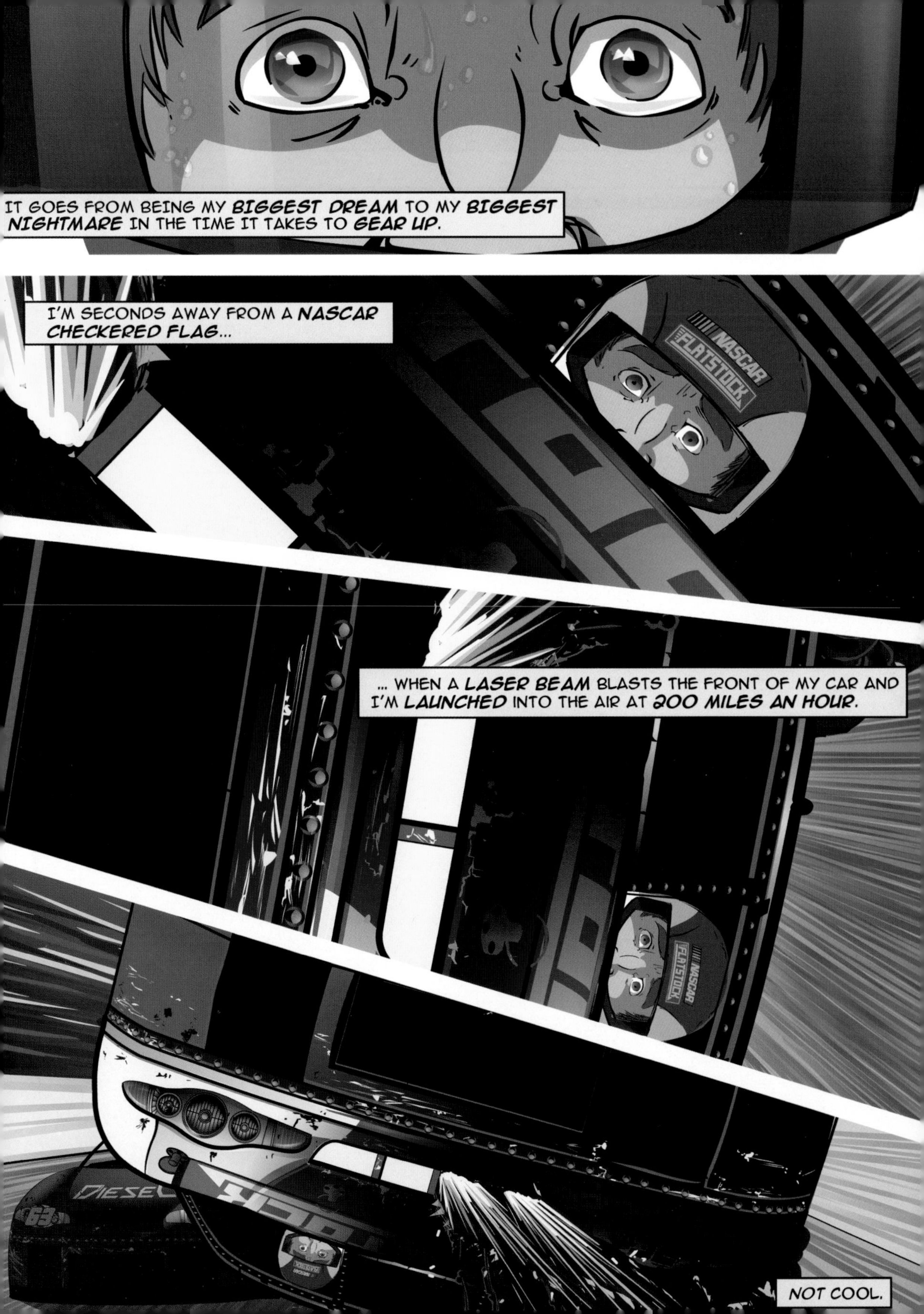
IT GOES FROM BEING MY BIGGEST DREAM TO MY BIGGEST NIGHTMARE IN THE TIME IT TAKES TO GEAR UP.
I'M SECONDS AWAY FROM A NASCAR CHECKERED FLAG...
NASCAR
FLATSTOCK
... WHEN A LASER BEAM BLASTS THE FRONT OF MY CAR AND I'M LAUNCHED INTO THE AIR AT 200 MILES AN HOUR.
NASCAR
FLATSTOCK
NOT COOL.

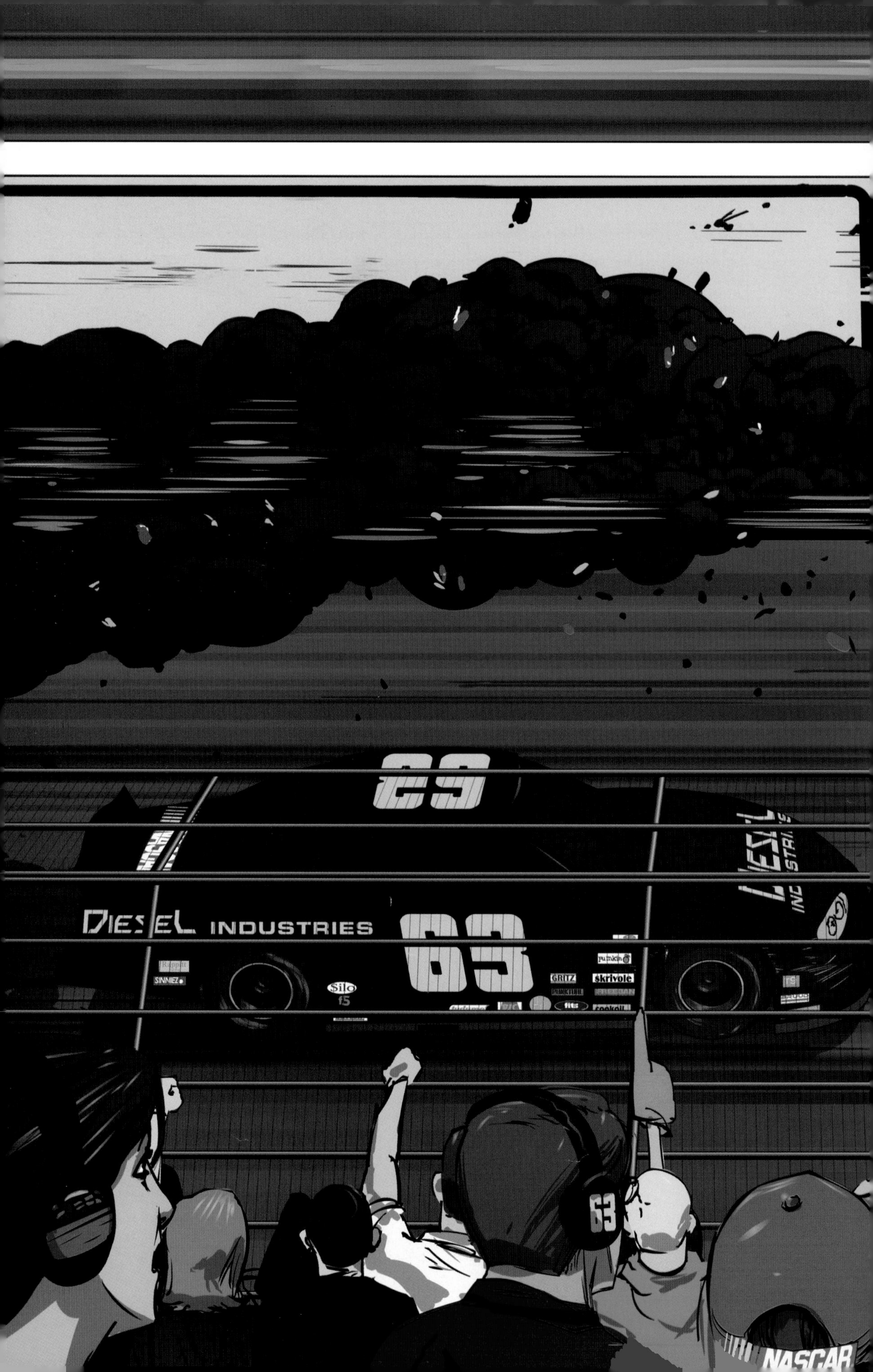
63
DIESEL INDUSTRIES
63
NASCAR

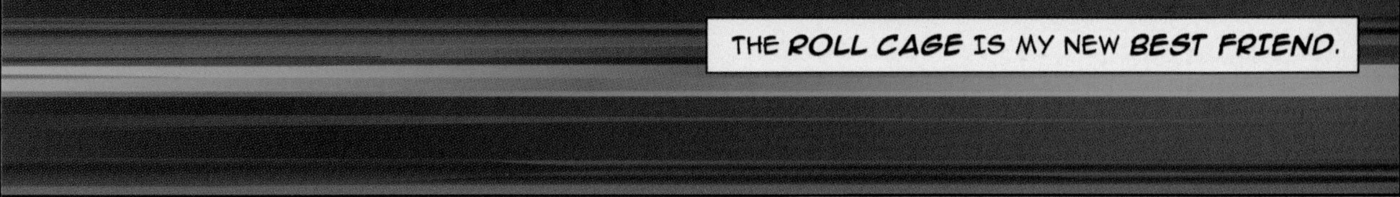
THE ROLL CAGE IS MY NEW BEST FRIEND.

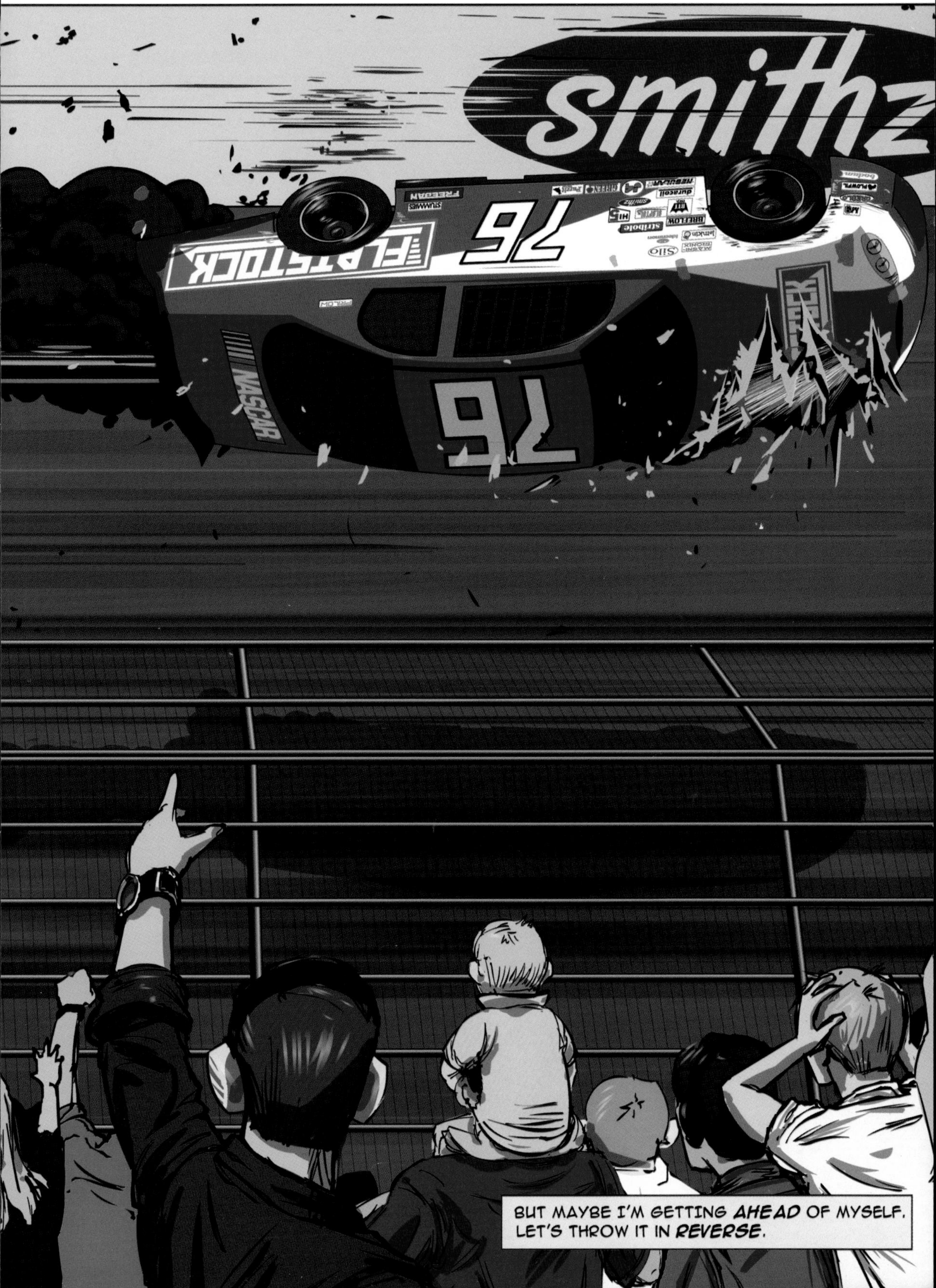
smithz
76
FLATSTOCK
NASCAR
76
BUT MAYBE I'M GETTING AHEAD OF MYSELF. LET'S THROW IT IN REVERSE.

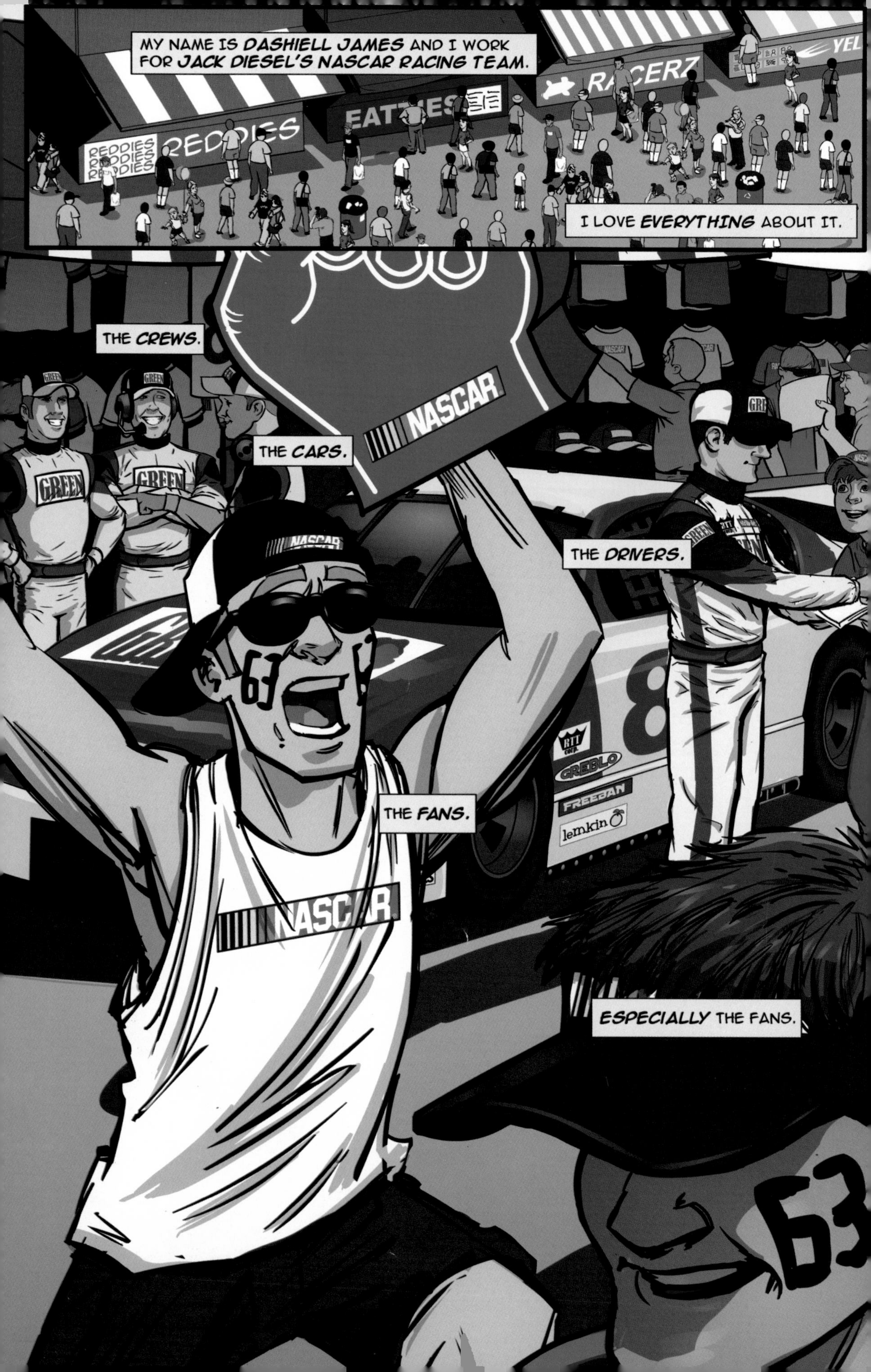
MY NAME IS DASHIELL JAMES AND I WORK FOR JACK DIESEL'S NASCAR RACING TEAM.
I LOVE EVERYTHING ABOUT IT.
THE CREWS.
THE CARS.
THE DRIVERS.
THE FANS.
ESPECIALLY THE FANS.

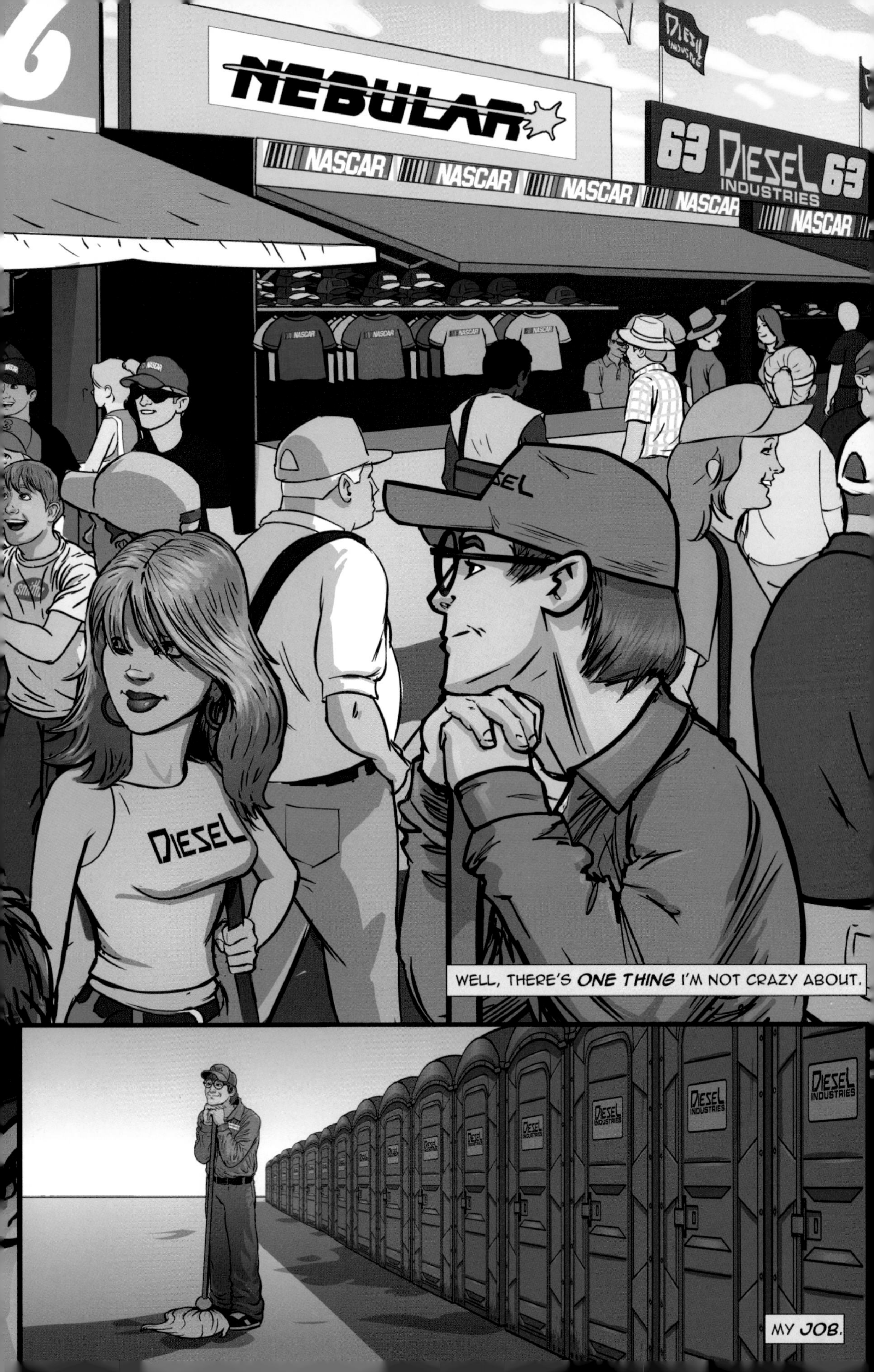

NEBULAR
NASCAR
63 DIESEL INDUSTRIES 63
DIESEL
WELL, THERE'S ONE THING I'M NOT CRAZY ABOUT.
DIESEL INDUSTRIES
MY JOB.

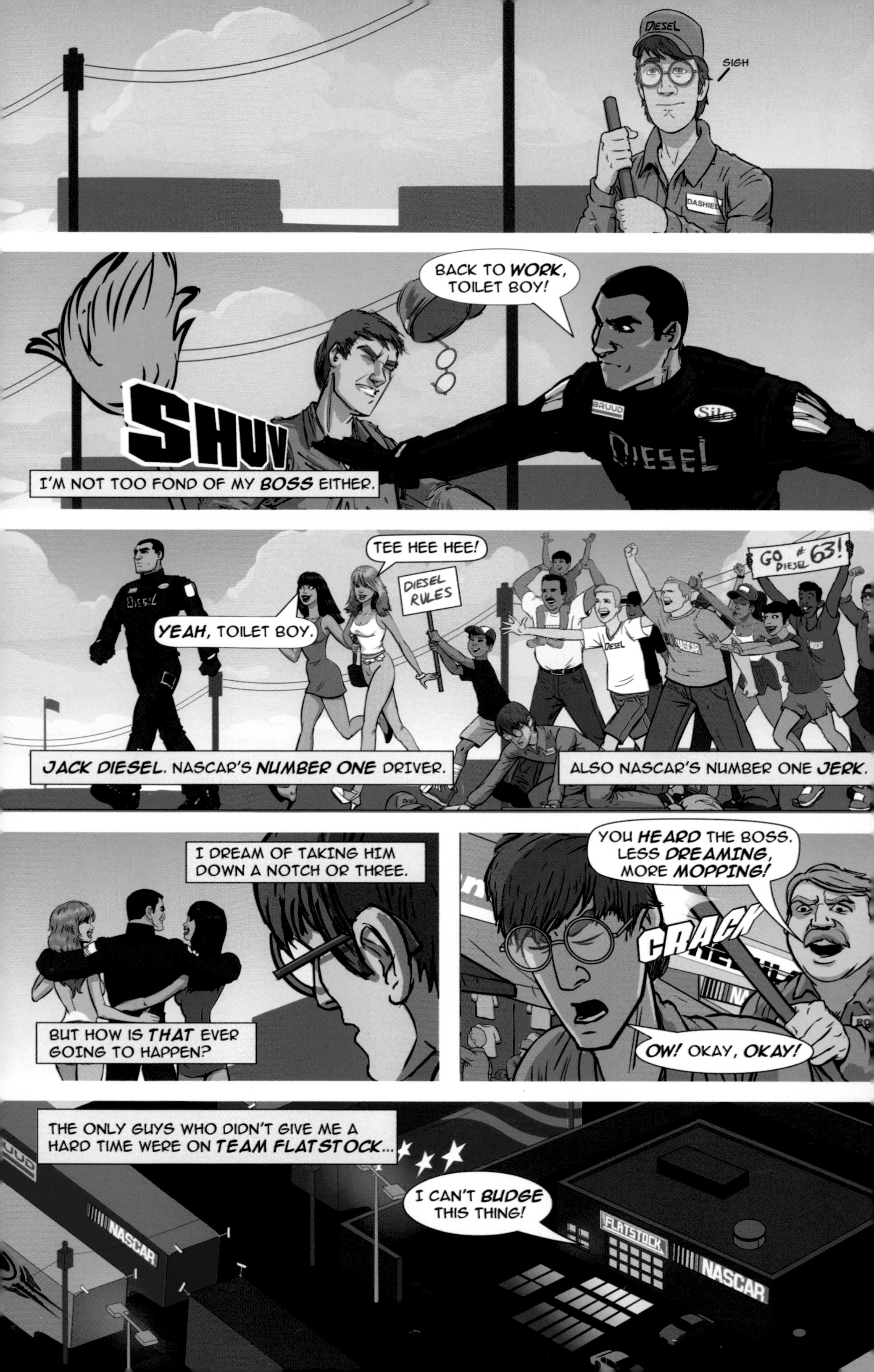

SIGH
DIESEL
DASHIELL
BACK TO WORK, TOILET BOY!
SHUV
I'M NOT TOO FOND OF MY BOSS EITHER.
BRUUD
DIESEL
TEE HEE HEE!
YEAH, TOILET BOY.
DIESEL RULES
GO DIESEL #63!
JACK DIESEL. NASCAR'S NUMBER ONE DRIVER.
ALSO NASCAR'S NUMBER ONE JERK.
I DREAM OF TAKING HIM DOWN A NOTCH OR THREE.
BUT HOW IS THAT EVER GOING TO HAPPEN?
YOU HEARD THE BOSS. LESS DREAMING, MORE MOPPING!
CRACK
OW! OKAY, OKAY!
THE ONLY GUYS WHO DIDN'T GIVE ME A HARD TIME WERE ON TEAM FLATSTOCK...
I CAN'T BUDGE THIS THING!
NASCAR
FLATSTOCK
NASCAR

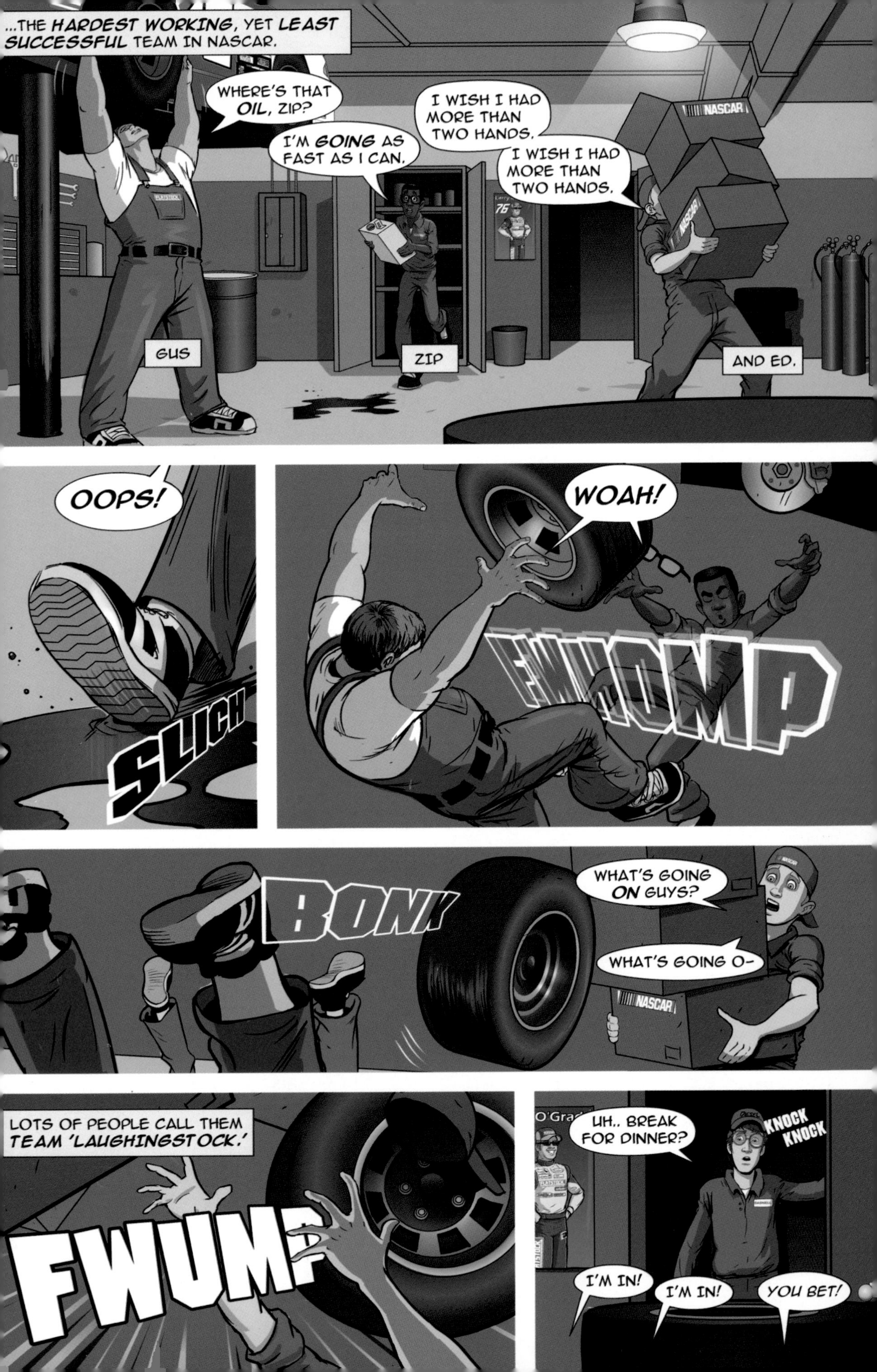
...THE HARDEST WORKING, YET LEAST SUCCESSFUL TEAM IN NASCAR.
WHERE'S THAT OIL, ZIP?
I'M GOING AS FAST AS I CAN.
I WISH I HAD MORE THAN TWO HANDS.
I WISH I HAD MORE THAN TWO HANDS.
GUS
ZIP
AND ED.
OOPS!
SLICH
WOAH!
BONK
WHAT'S GOING ON GUYS?
WHAT'S GOING O-
LOTS OF PEOPLE CALL THEM TEAM 'LAUGHINGSTOCK.'
FWUMP
UH.. BREAK FOR DINNER?
KNOCK KNOCK
I'M IN!
I'M IN!
YOU BET!

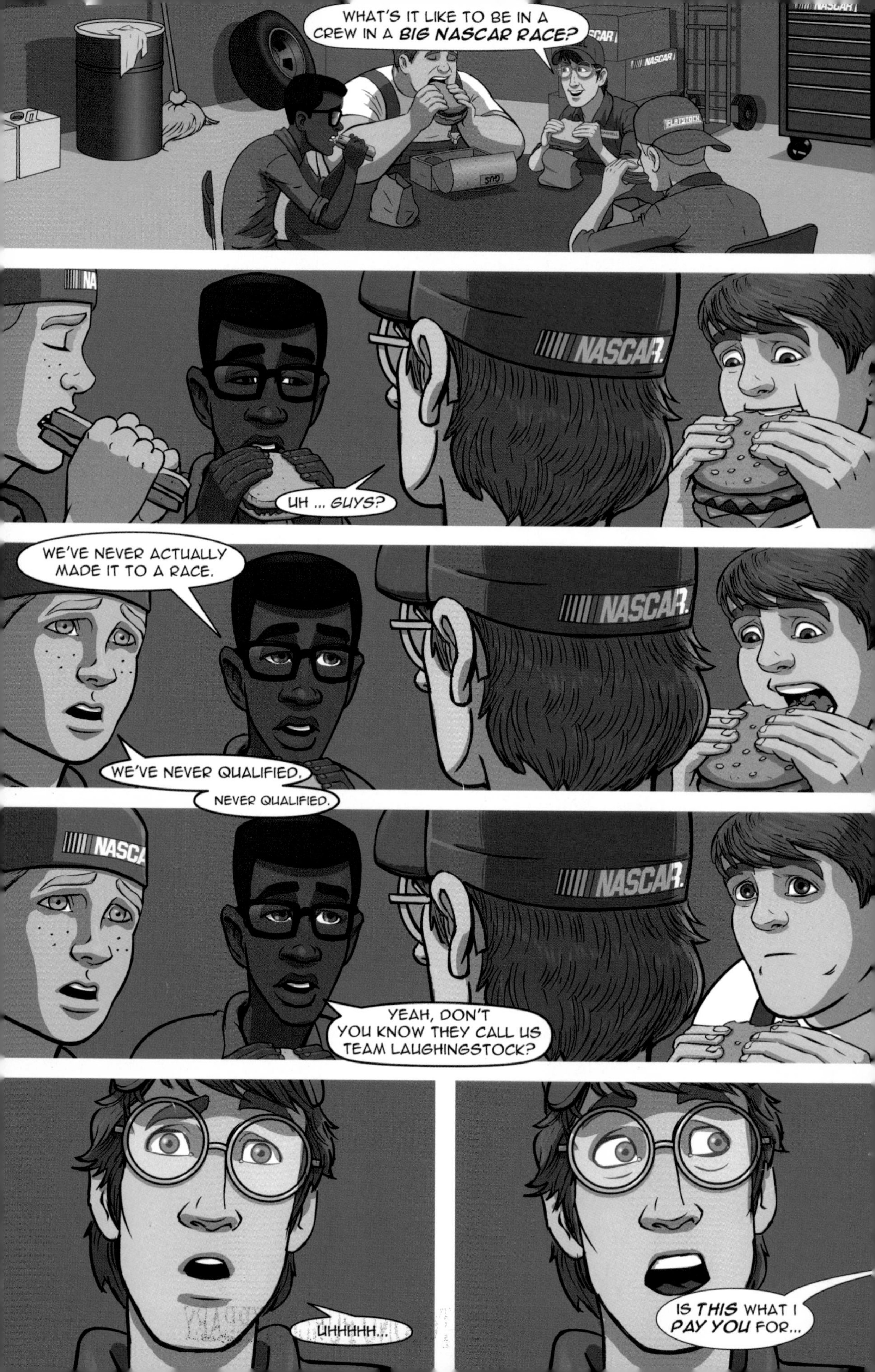
WHAT'S IT LIKE TO BE IN A CREW IN A BIG NASCAR RACE?
UH ... GUYS?
WE'VE NEVER ACTUALLY MADE IT TO A RACE.
WE'VE NEVER QUALIFIED.
NEVER QUALIFIED.
YEAH, DON'T YOU KNOW THEY CALL US TEAM LAUGHINGSTOCK?
UHHHHH...
IS THIS WHAT I PAY YOU FOR...

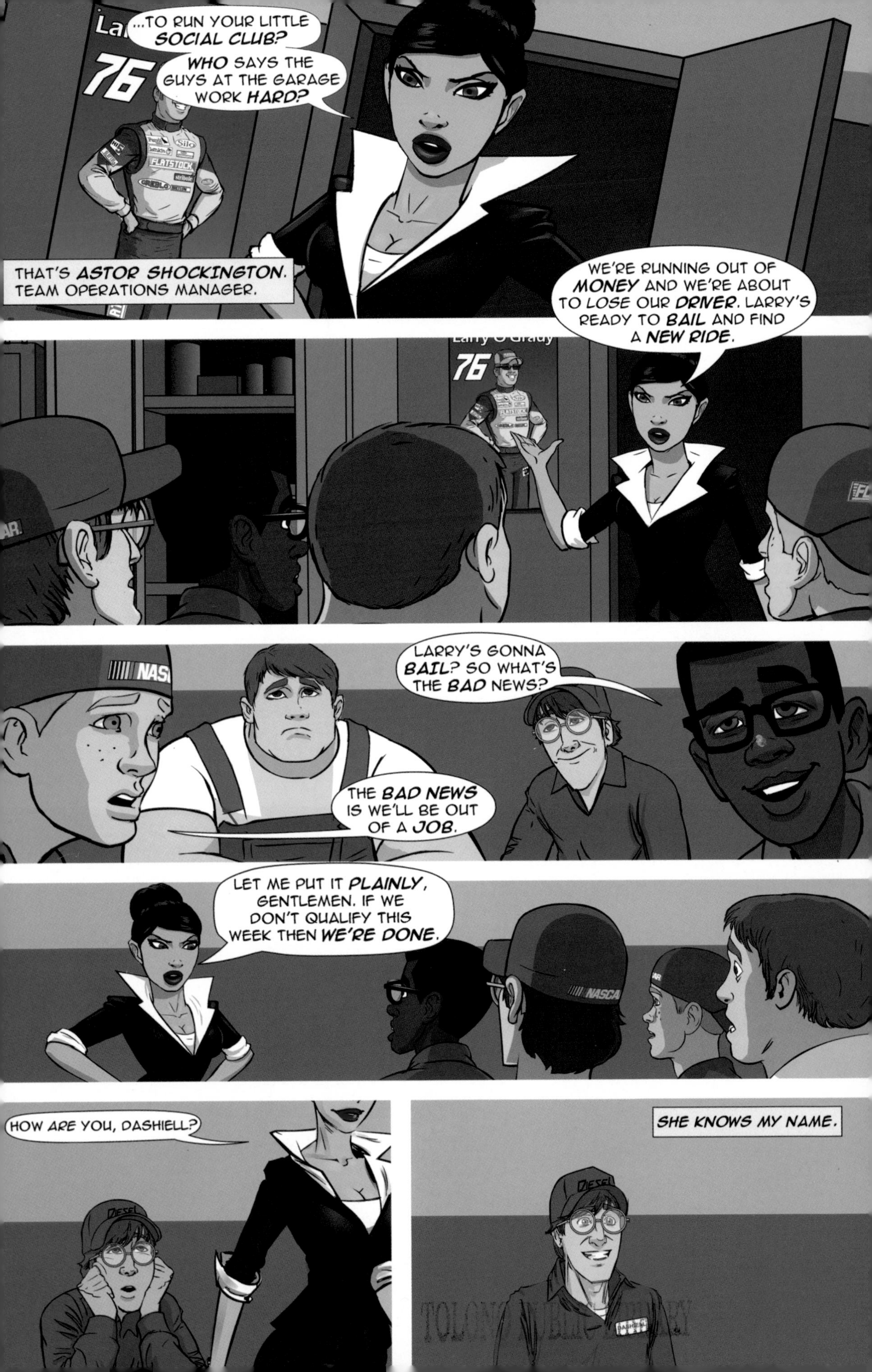
...TO RUN YOUR LITTLE SOCIAL CLUB?
WHO SAYS THE GUYS AT THE GARAGE WORK HARD?
THAT'S ASTOR SHOCKINGTON. TEAM OPERATIONS MANAGER.
WE'RE RUNNING OUT OF MONEY AND WE'RE ABOUT TO LOSE OUR DRIVER. LARRY'S READY TO BAIL AND FIND A NEW RIDE.
76
LARRY'S GONNA BAIL? SO WHAT'S THE BAD NEWS?
THE BAD NEWS IS WE'LL BE OUT OF A JOB.
LET ME PUT IT PLAINLY, GENTLEMEN. IF WE DON'T QUALIFY THIS WEEK THEN WE'RE DONE.
HOW ARE YOU, DASHIELL?
SHE KNOWS MY NAME.

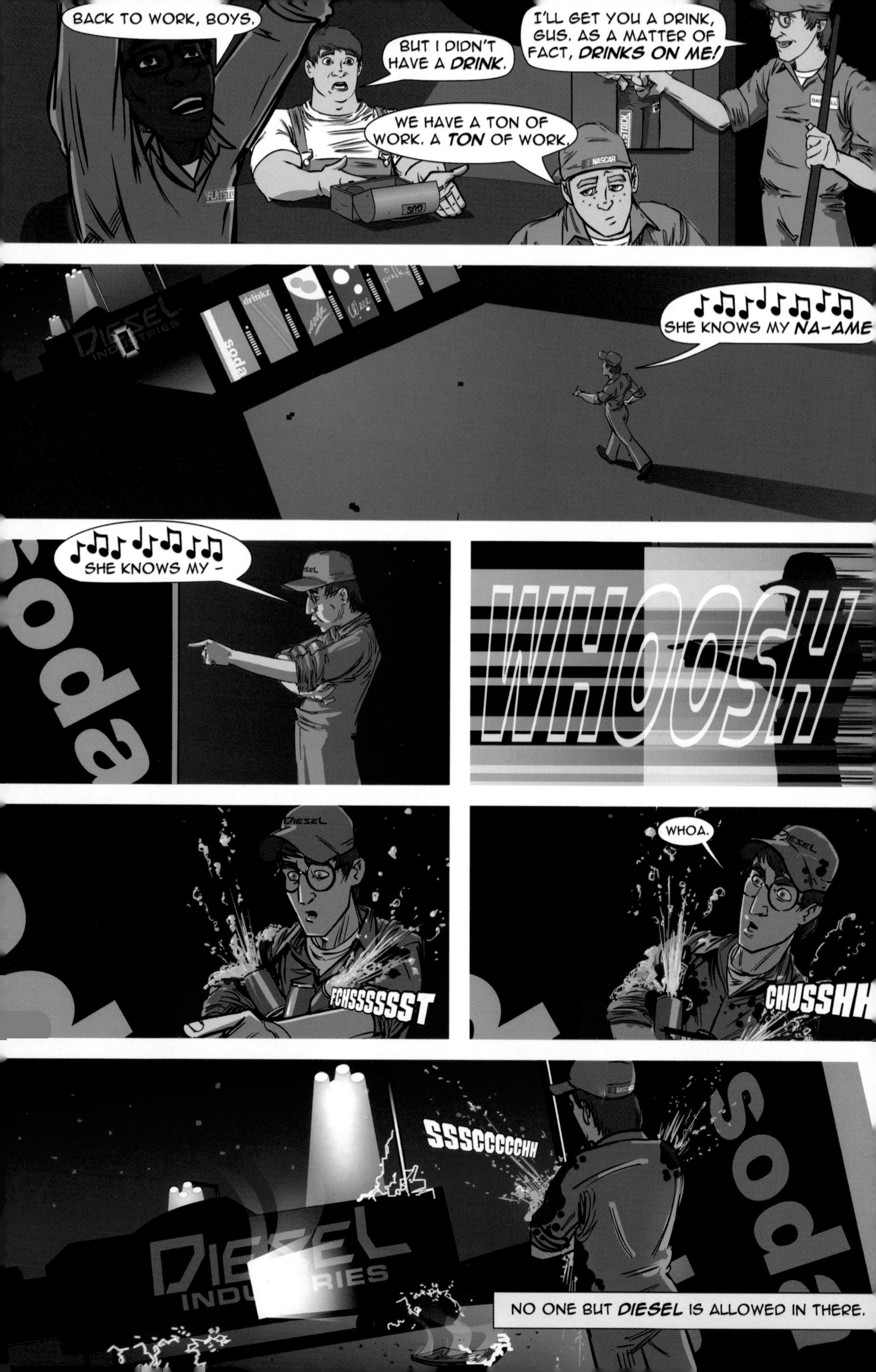
BACK TO WORK, BOYS.
BUT I DIDN'T HAVE A DRINK.
I'LL GET YOU A DRINK, GUS. AS A MATTER OF FACT, DRINKS ON ME!
WE HAVE A TON OF WORK. A TON OF WORK.
FLATSTO
GUS
NASCAR
DIESEL INDUSTRIES
soda
drinkz
pink
SHE KNOWS MY NA-AME
SHE KNOWS MY -
soda
WHOOSH
FCHSSSSSST
WHOA.
CHUSSHH
SSSCCCCCHH
DIESEL INDUSTRIES
soda
NO ONE BUT DIESEL IS ALLOWED IN THERE.

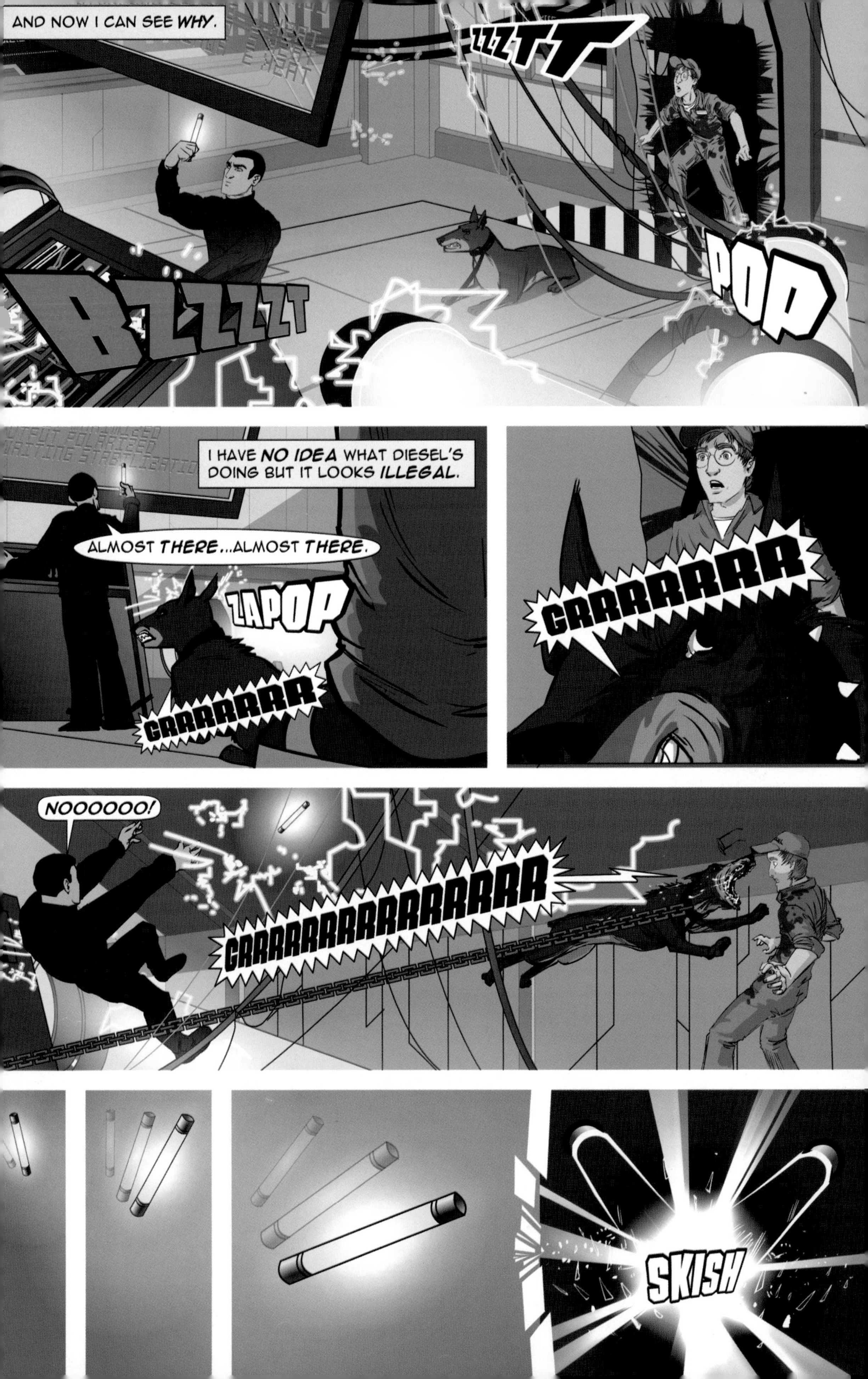
AND NOW I CAN SEE WHY.
ZZZTT
BZZZZZT
POP
I HAVE NO IDEA WHAT DIESEL'S DOING BUT IT LOOKS ILLEGAL.
ALMOST THERE...ALMOST THERE.
ZAPOP
GRRRRRRR
GRRRRRRR
NOOOOOO!
GRRRRRRRRRRRRRRR
SKISH

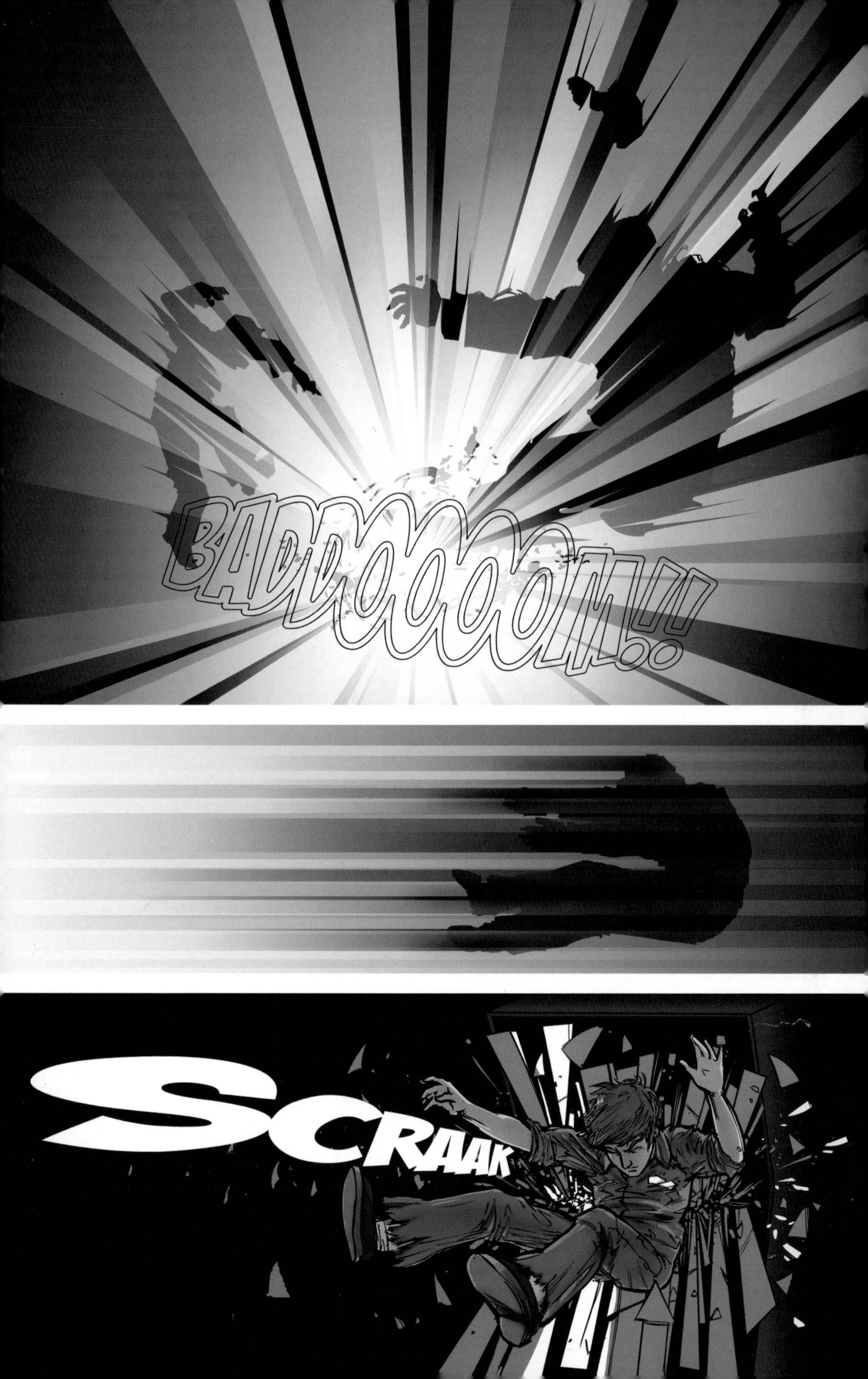
BADDOOOOM!!
SCRAAK

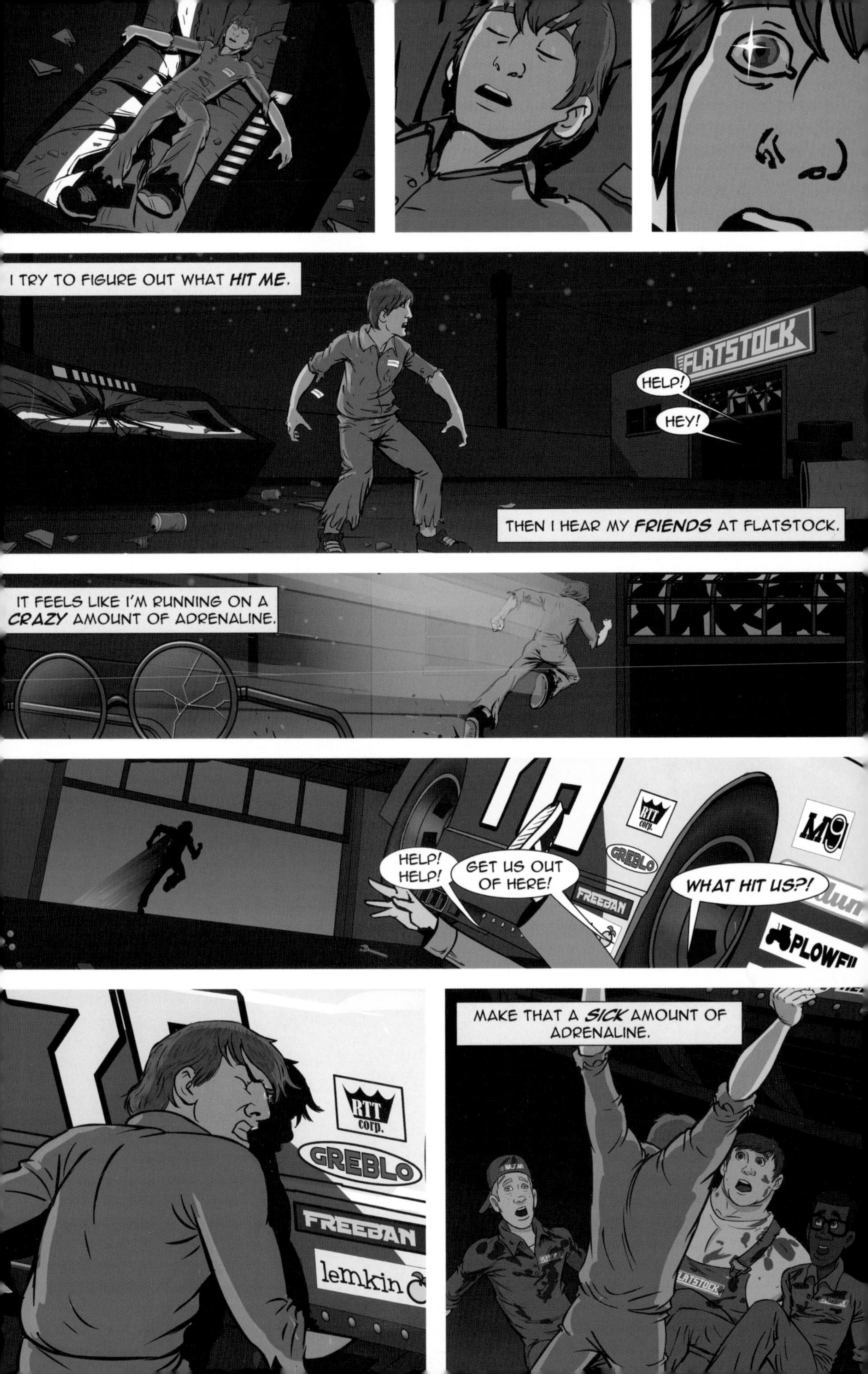
I TRY TO FIGURE OUT WHAT *HIT ME*.
FLATSTOCK
HELP!
HEY!
THEN I HEAR MY *FRIENDS* AT FLATSTOCK.
IT FEELS LIKE I'M RUNNING ON A *CRAZY* AMOUNT OF ADRENALINE.
RTT corp.
GREBLO
FREEBAN
HELP! HELP!
GET US OUT OF HERE!
WHAT HIT US?!
PLOWF
MAKE THAT A *SICK* AMOUNT OF ADRENALINE.
RTT corp.
GREBLO
FREEBAN
lemkin

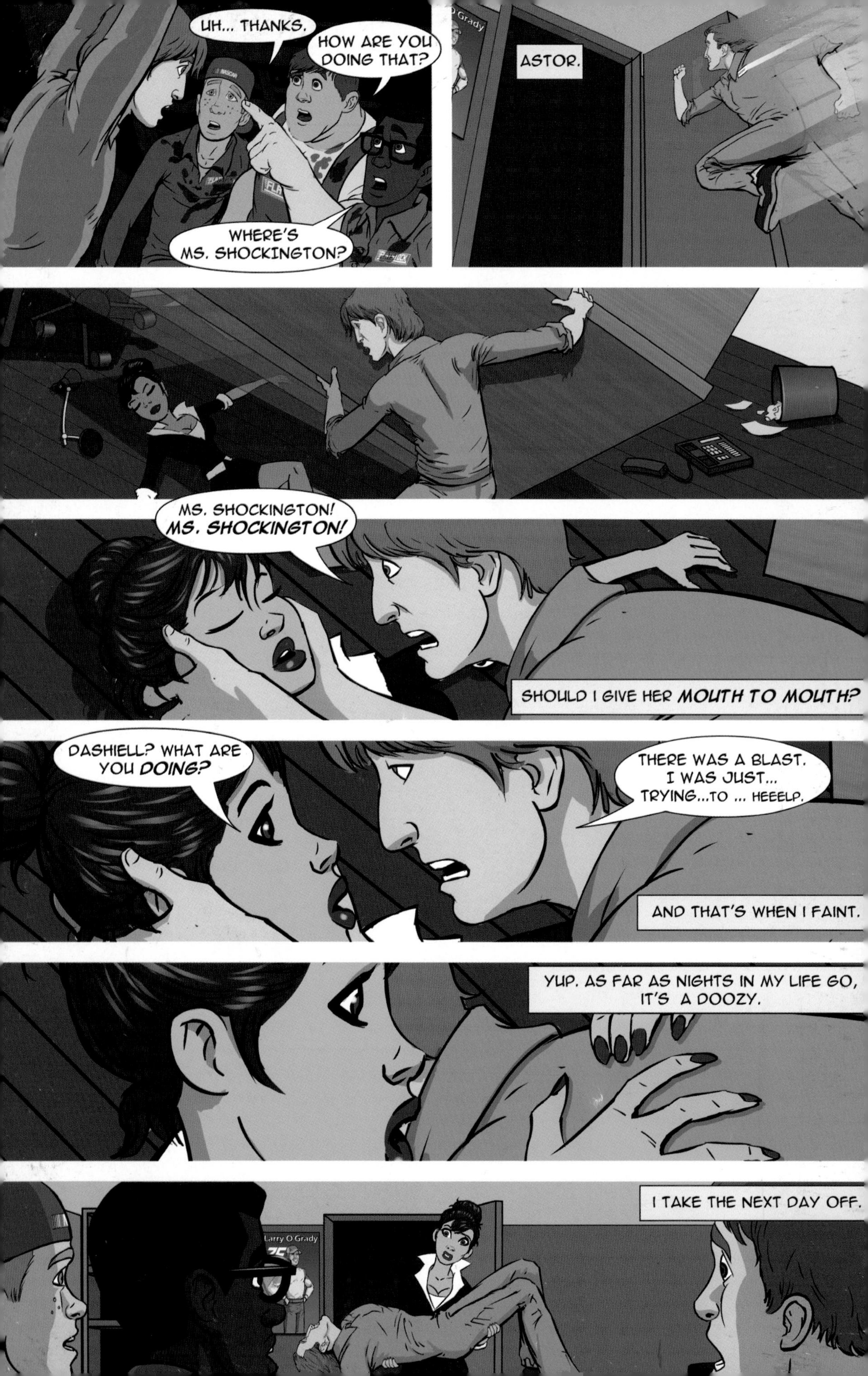

UH... THANKS.
HOW ARE YOU DOING THAT?
WHERE'S MS. SHOCKINGTON?
ASTOR.
MS. SHOCKINGTON! ***MS. SHOCKINGTON!***
SHOULD I GIVE HER ***MOUTH TO MOUTH?***
DASHIELL? WHAT ARE YOU ***DOING?***
THERE WAS A BLAST. I WAS JUST... TRYING...TO ... HEEELP.
AND THAT'S WHEN I FAINT.
YUP. AS FAR AS NIGHTS IN MY LIFE GO, IT'S A DOOZY.
I TAKE THE NEXT DAY OFF.

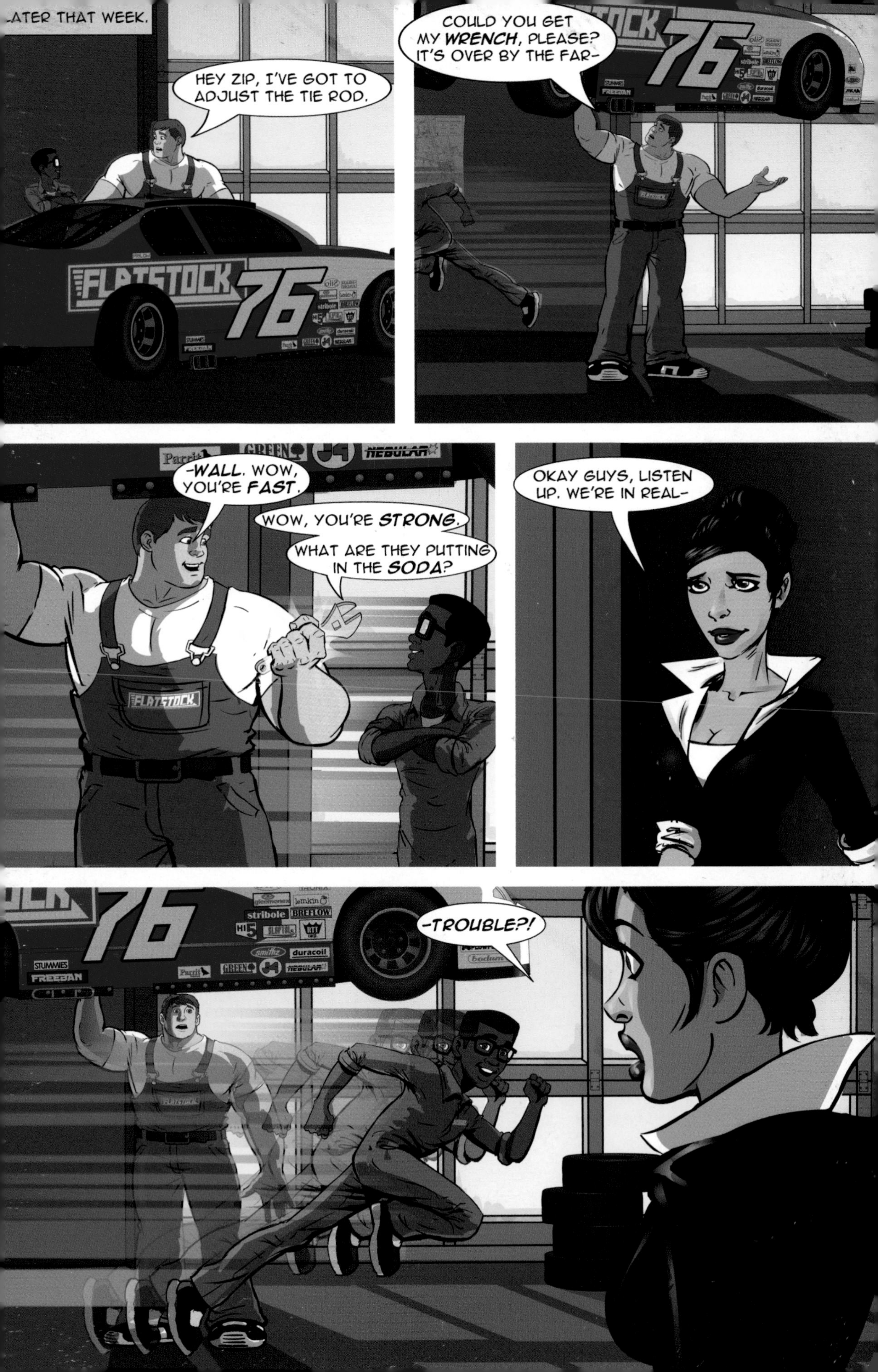

-ATER THAT WEEK.
HEY ZIP, I'VE GOT TO ADJUST THE TIE ROD.
COULD YOU GET MY WRENCH, PLEASE? IT'S OVER BY THE FAR-
-WALL. WOW, YOU'RE FAST.
WOW, YOU'RE STRONG.
WHAT ARE THEY PUTTING IN THE SODA?
OKAY GUYS, LISTEN UP. WE'RE IN REAL-
-TROUBLE?!

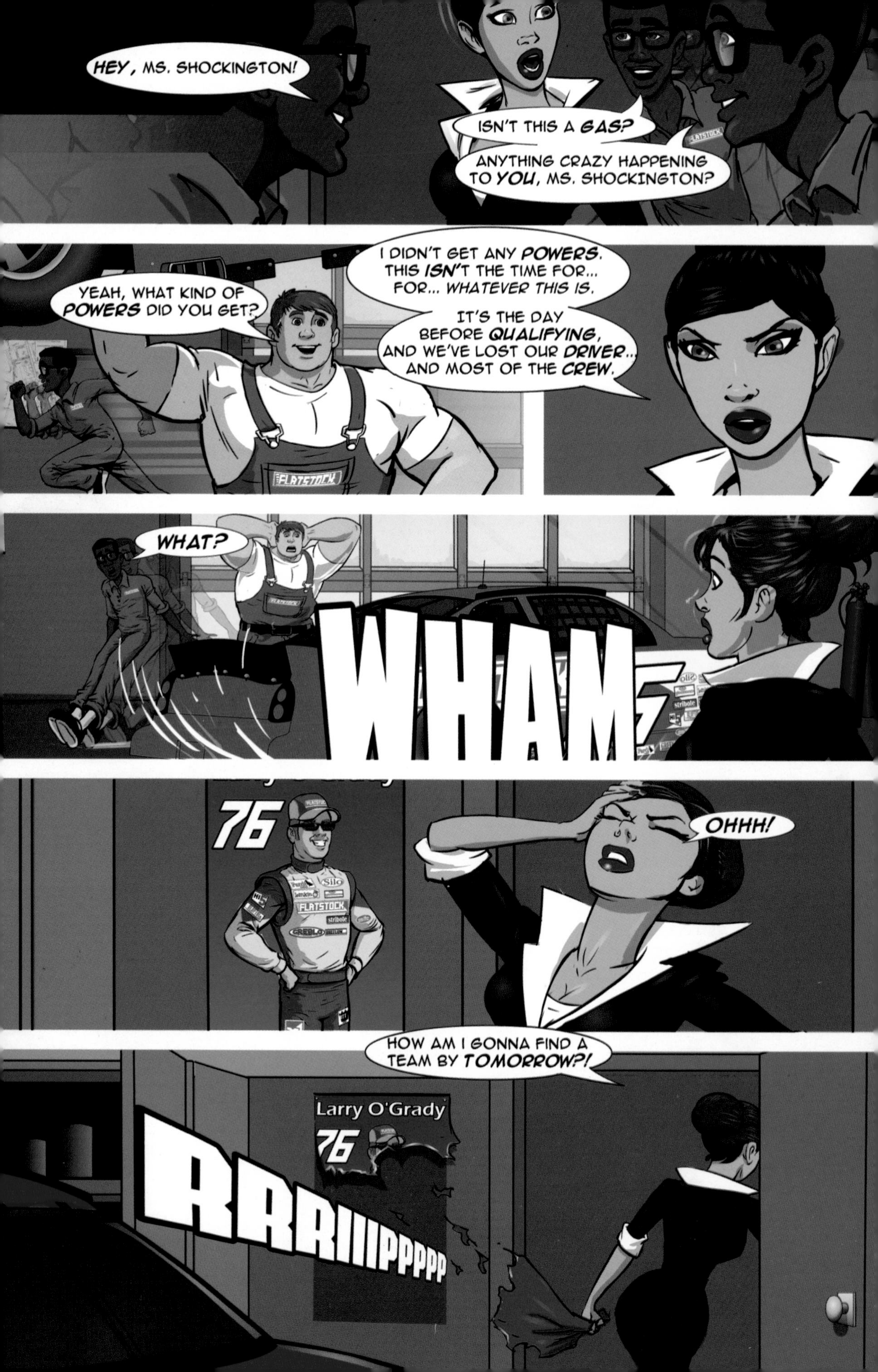

HEY, MS. SHOCKINGTON!
ISN'T THIS A GAS?
ANYTHING CRAZY HAPPENING TO YOU, MS. SHOCKINGTON?
YEAH, WHAT KIND OF POWERS DID YOU GET?
I DIDN'T GET ANY POWERS. THIS ISN'T THE TIME FOR... FOR... WHATEVER THIS IS.
IT'S THE DAY BEFORE QUALIFYING, AND WE'VE LOST OUR DRIVER... AND MOST OF THE CREW.
WHAT?
WHAM
76
OHHH!
HOW AM I GONNA FIND A TEAM BY TOMORROW?!
Larry O'Grady
76
RRRIIIPPPPP

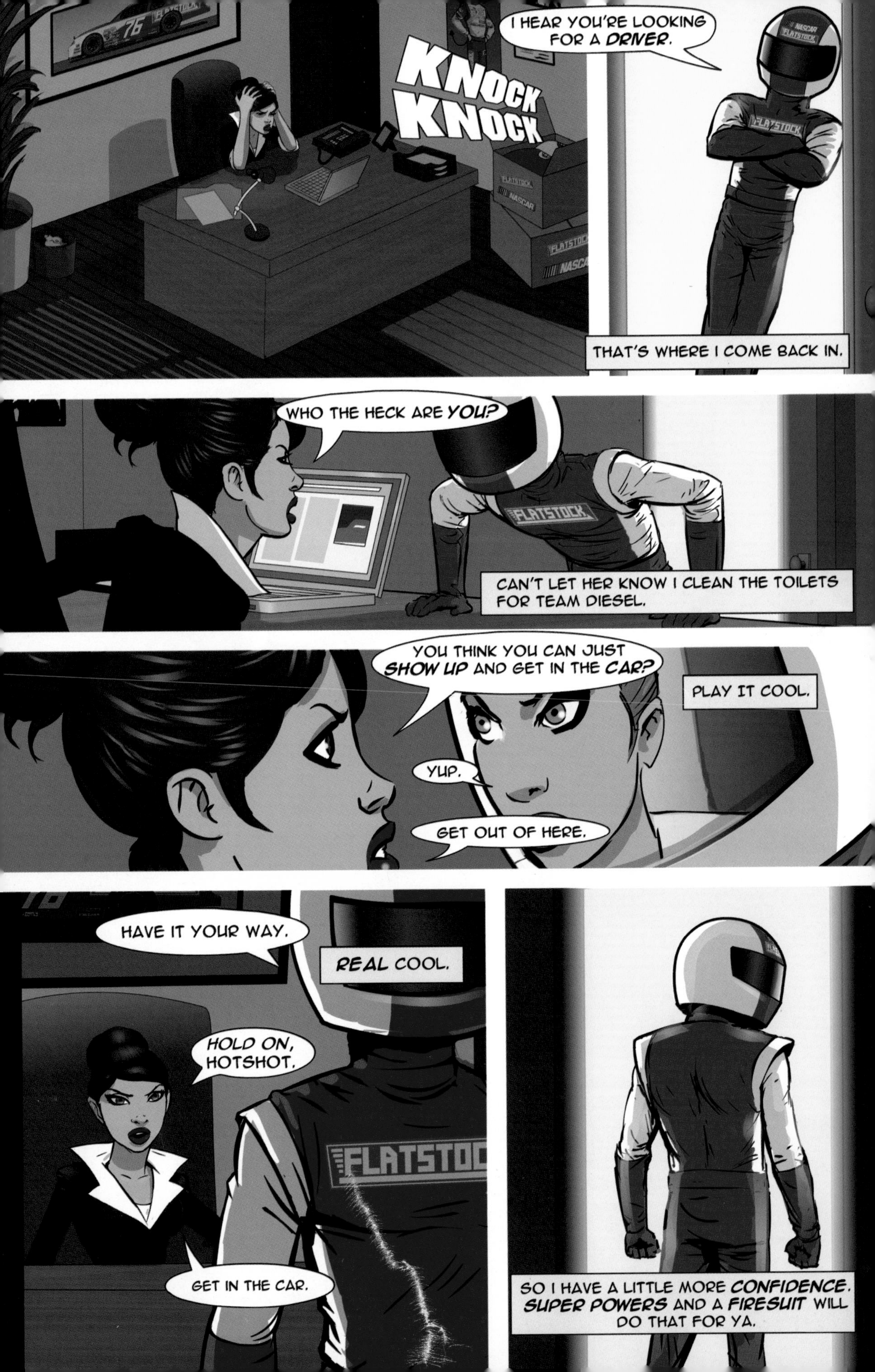
KNOCK KNOCK
I HEAR YOU'RE LOOKING FOR A DRIVER.
THAT'S WHERE I COME BACK IN.
WHO THE HECK ARE YOU?
CAN'T LET HER KNOW I CLEAN THE TOILETS FOR TEAM DIESEL.
YOU THINK YOU CAN JUST SHOW UP AND GET IN THE CAR?
PLAY IT COOL.
YUP.
GET OUT OF HERE.
HAVE IT YOUR WAY.
REAL COOL.
HOLD ON, HOTSHOT.
GET IN THE CAR.
SO I HAVE A LITTLE MORE CONFIDENCE. SUPER POWERS AND A FIRESUIT WILL DO THAT FOR YA.

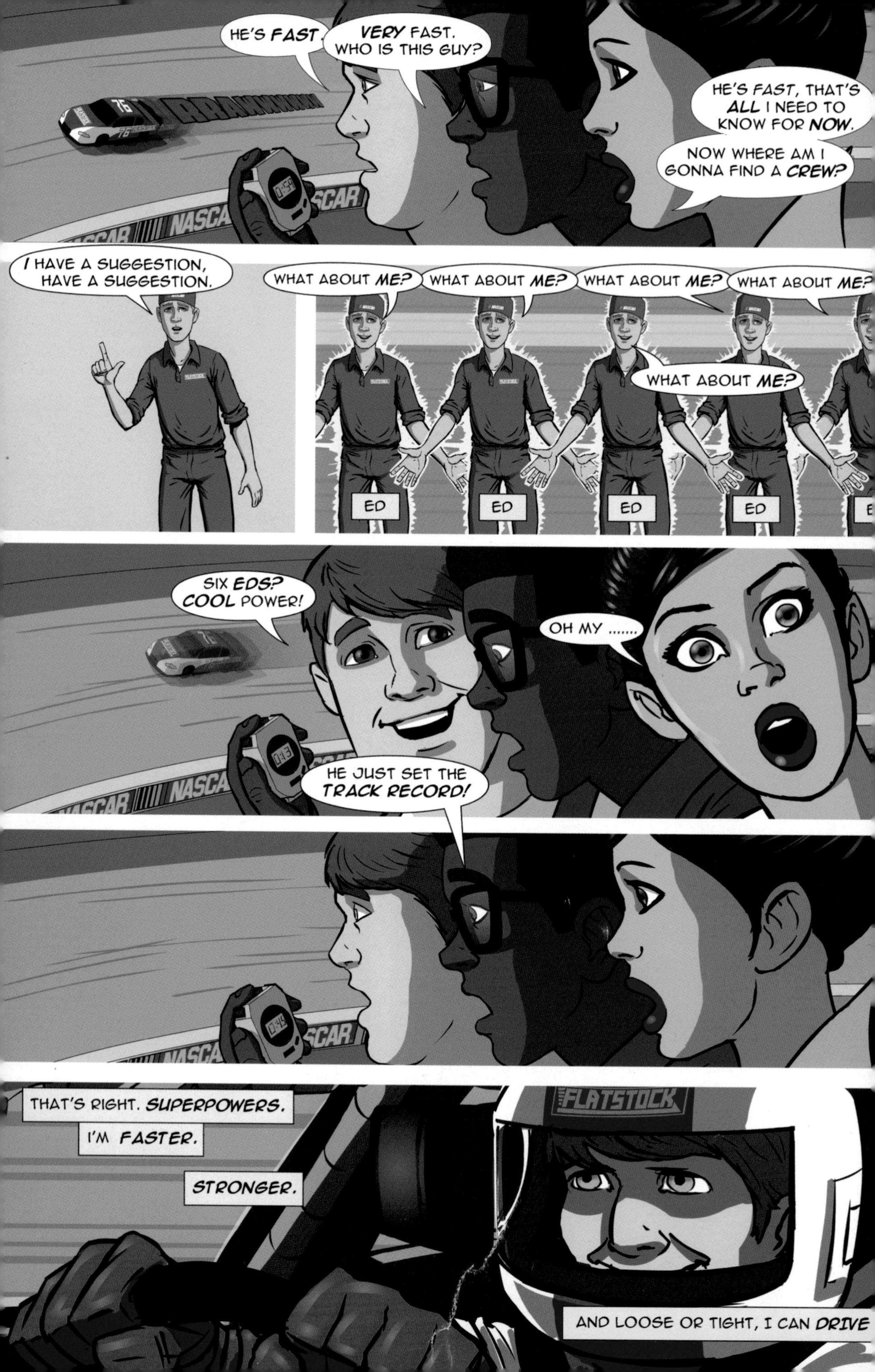

HE'S FAST.
VERY FAST. WHO IS THIS GUY?
HE'S FAST, THAT'S ALL I NEED TO KNOW FOR NOW.
NOW WHERE AM I GONNA FIND A CREW?
I HAVE A SUGGESTION, HAVE A SUGGESTION.
WHAT ABOUT ME?
WHAT ABOUT ME?
WHAT ABOUT ME?
WHAT ABOUT ME?
WHAT ABOUT ME?
ED
ED
ED
ED
SIX EDS? COOL POWER!
OH MY ....
HE JUST SET THE TRACK RECORD!
THAT'S RIGHT. SUPERPOWERS.
I'M FASTER.
STRONGER.
AND LOOSE OR TIGHT, I CAN DRIVE

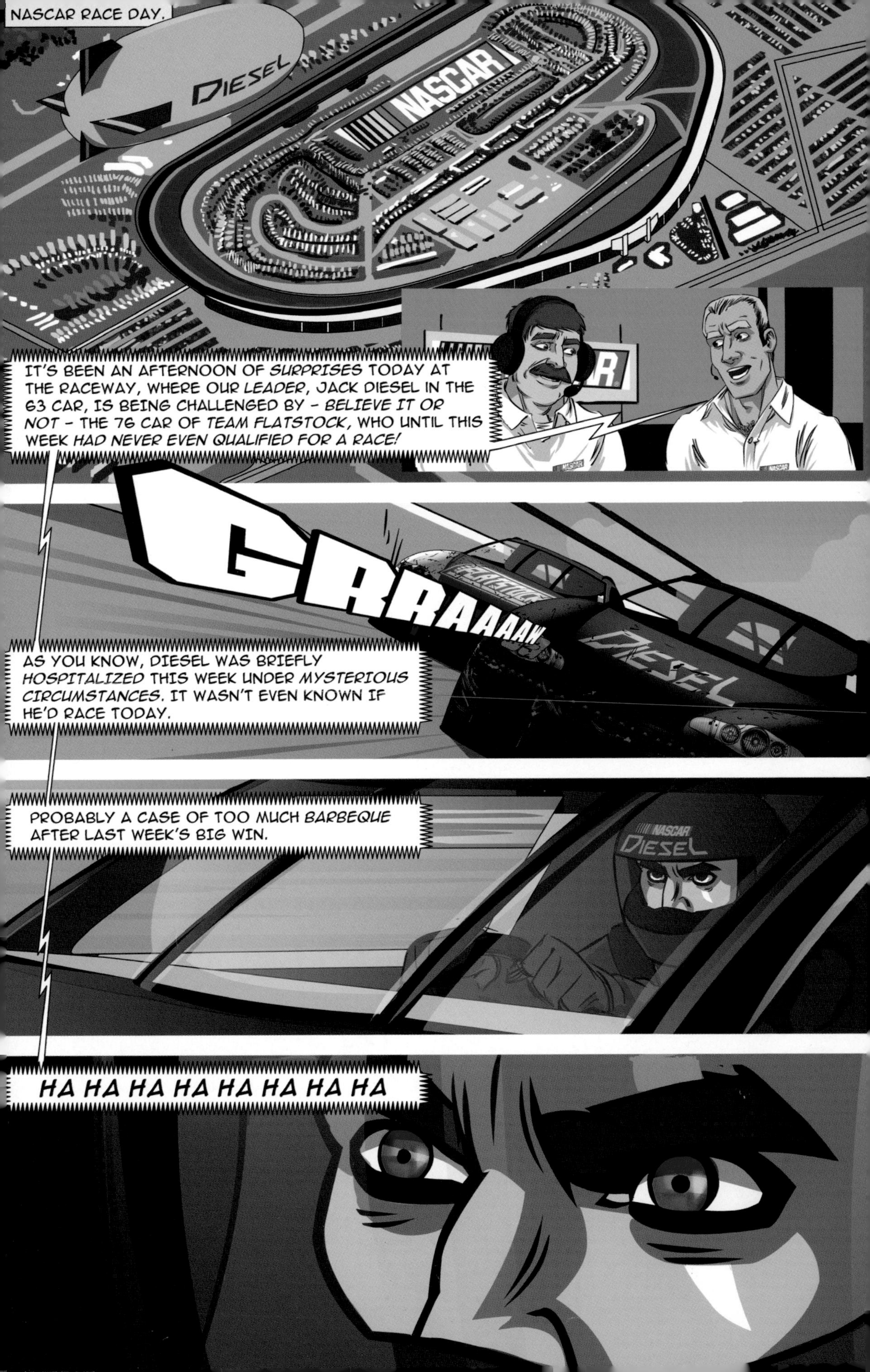
NASCAR RACE DAY.
DIESEL
NASCAR
IT'S BEEN AN AFTERNOON OF SURPRISES TODAY AT THE RACEWAY, WHERE OUR LEADER, JACK DIESEL IN THE 63 CAR, IS BEING CHALLENGED BY – BELIEVE IT OR NOT – THE 76 CAR OF TEAM FLATSTOCK, WHO UNTIL THIS WEEK HAD NEVER EVEN QUALIFIED FOR A RACE!
GRRAAAAW
DIESEL
AS YOU KNOW, DIESEL WAS BRIEFLY HOSPITALIZED THIS WEEK UNDER MYSTERIOUS CIRCUMSTANCES. IT WASN'T EVEN KNOWN IF HE'D RACE TODAY.
PROBABLY A CASE OF TOO MUCH BARBEQUE AFTER LAST WEEK'S BIG WIN.
NASCAR
DIESEL
HA HA HA HA HA HA HA HA

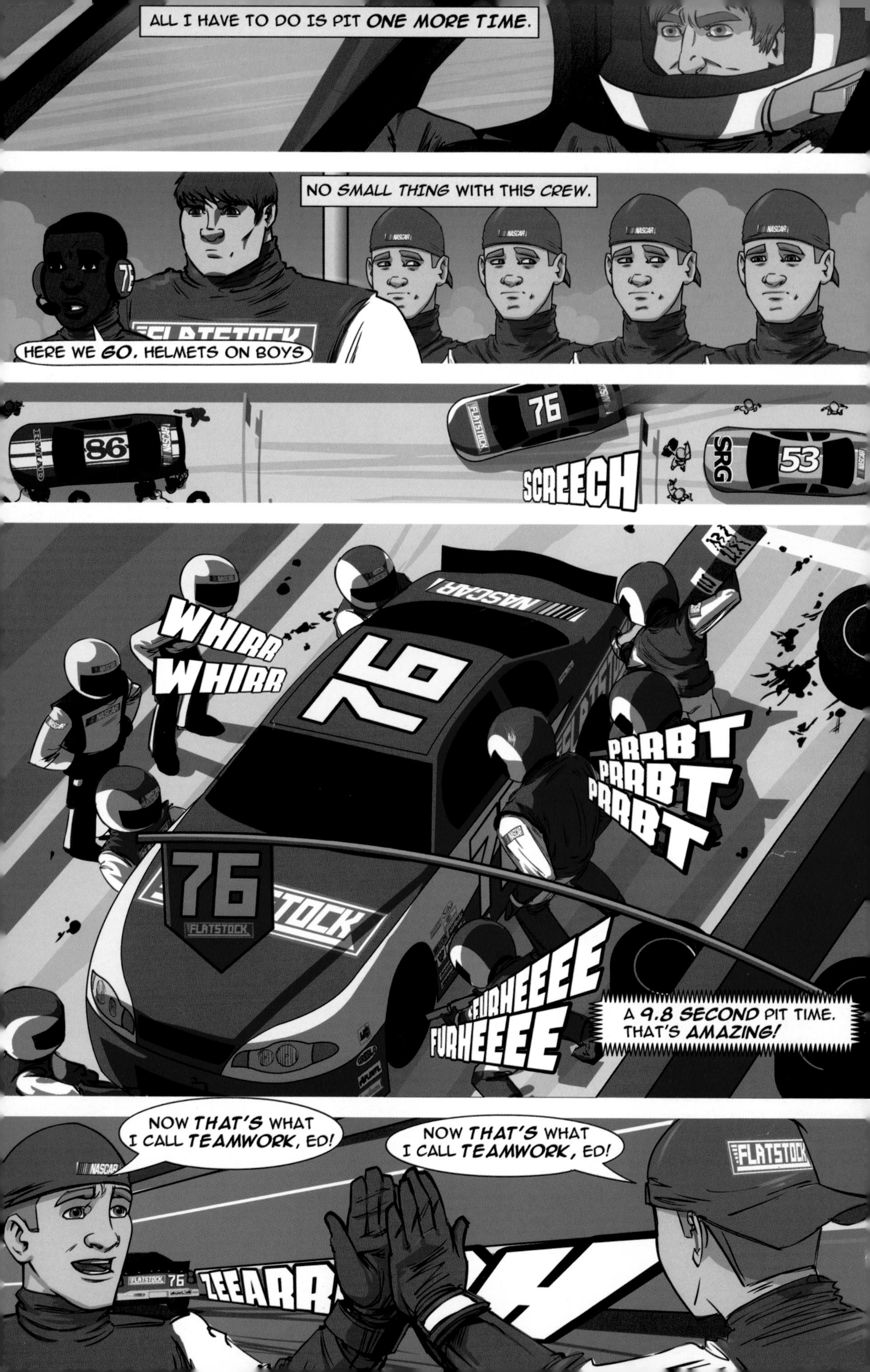
ALL I HAVE TO DO IS PIT ONE MORE TIME.
NO SMALL THING WITH THIS CREW.
HERE WE GO. HELMETS ON BOYS
SCREECH
WHIRR
WHIRR
PRRBT
PRRBT
PRRBT
FURHEEEE
FURHEEEE
A 9.8 SECOND PIT TIME. THAT'S AMAZING!
NOW THAT'S WHAT I CALL TEAMWORK, ED!
NOW THAT'S WHAT I CALL TEAMWORK, ED!

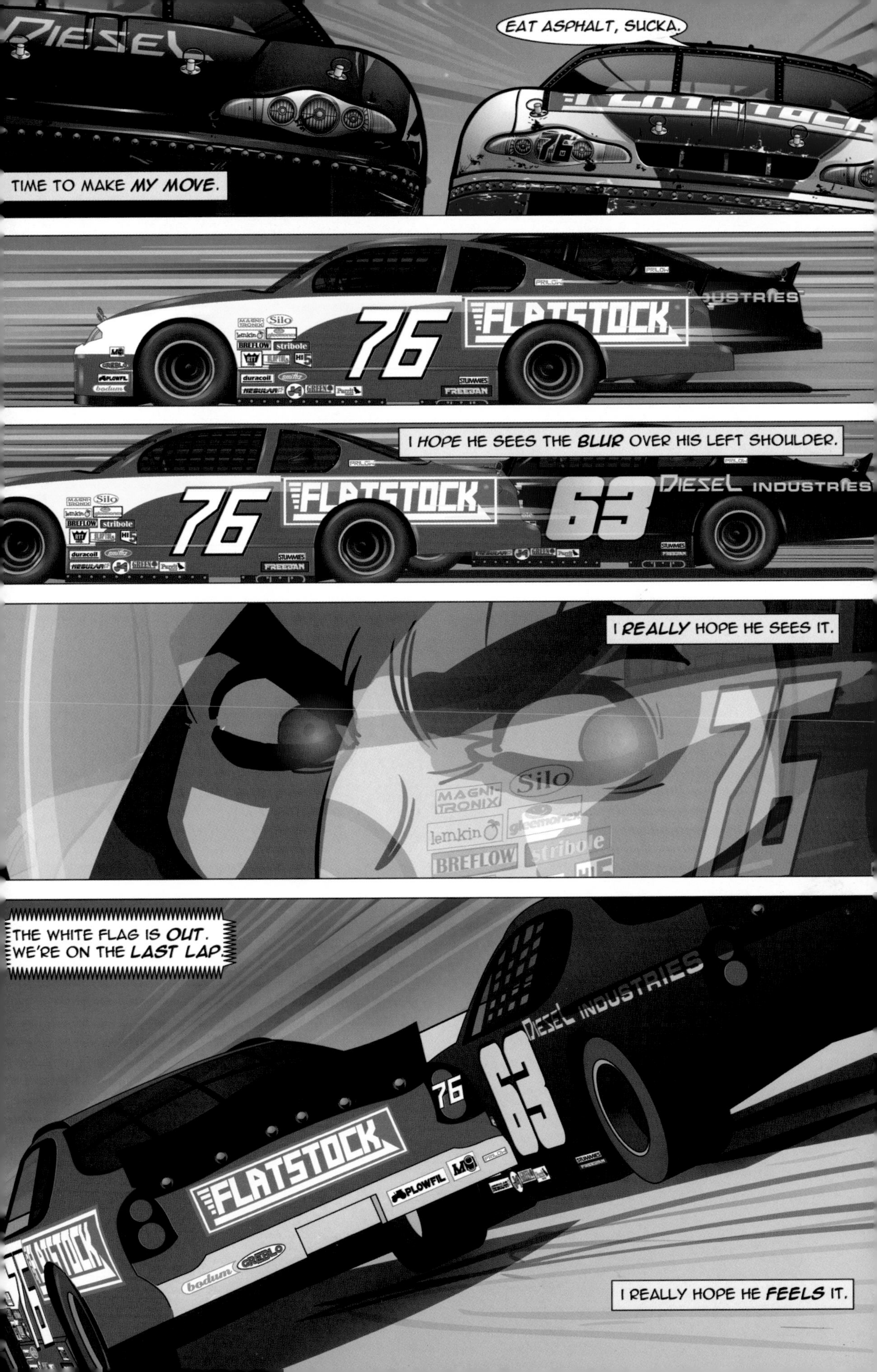
DIESEL
EAT ASPHALT, SUCKA.
FLATSTOCK
76
TIME TO MAKE MY MOVE.
76
FLATSTOCK
I HOPE HE SEES THE BLUR OVER HIS LEFT SHOULDER.
76
FLATSTOCK
63
DIESEL INDUSTRIES
I REALLY HOPE HE SEES IT.
MAGNI-TRONIX
Silo
lemkin
BREFLOW
stribole
THE WHITE FLAG IS OUT.
WE'RE ON THE LAST LAP.
DIESEL INDUSTRIES
63
76
FLATSTOCK
FLATSTOCK
PLOWFIL
bodum
GREBLO
I REALLY HOPE HE FEELS IT.

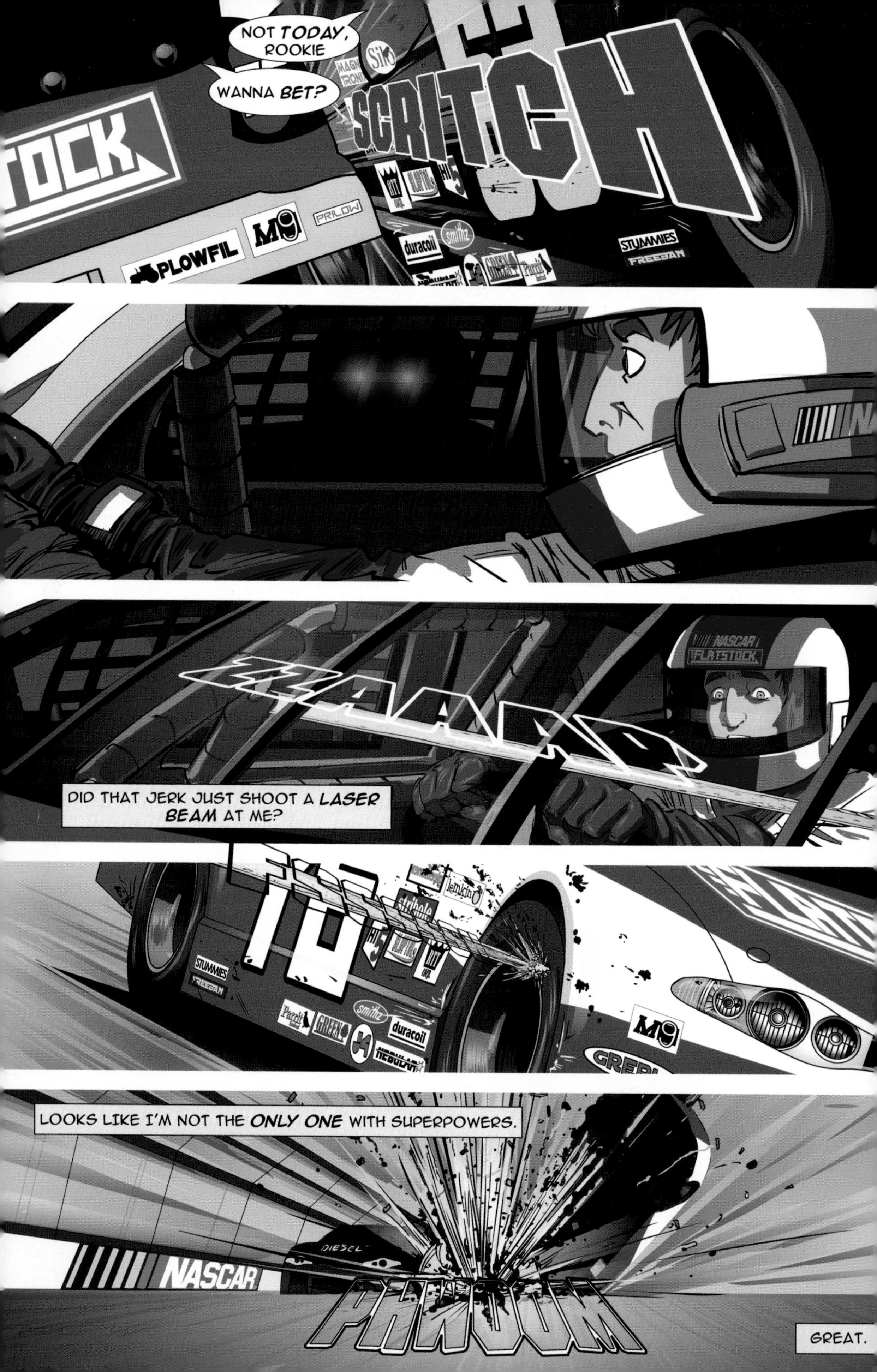
NOT TODAY, ROOKIE
WANNA BET?
SCRITCH
DID THAT JERK JUST SHOOT A LASER BEAM AT ME?
LOOKS LIKE I'M NOT THE ONLY ONE WITH SUPERPOWERS.
PHWOOM
GREAT.

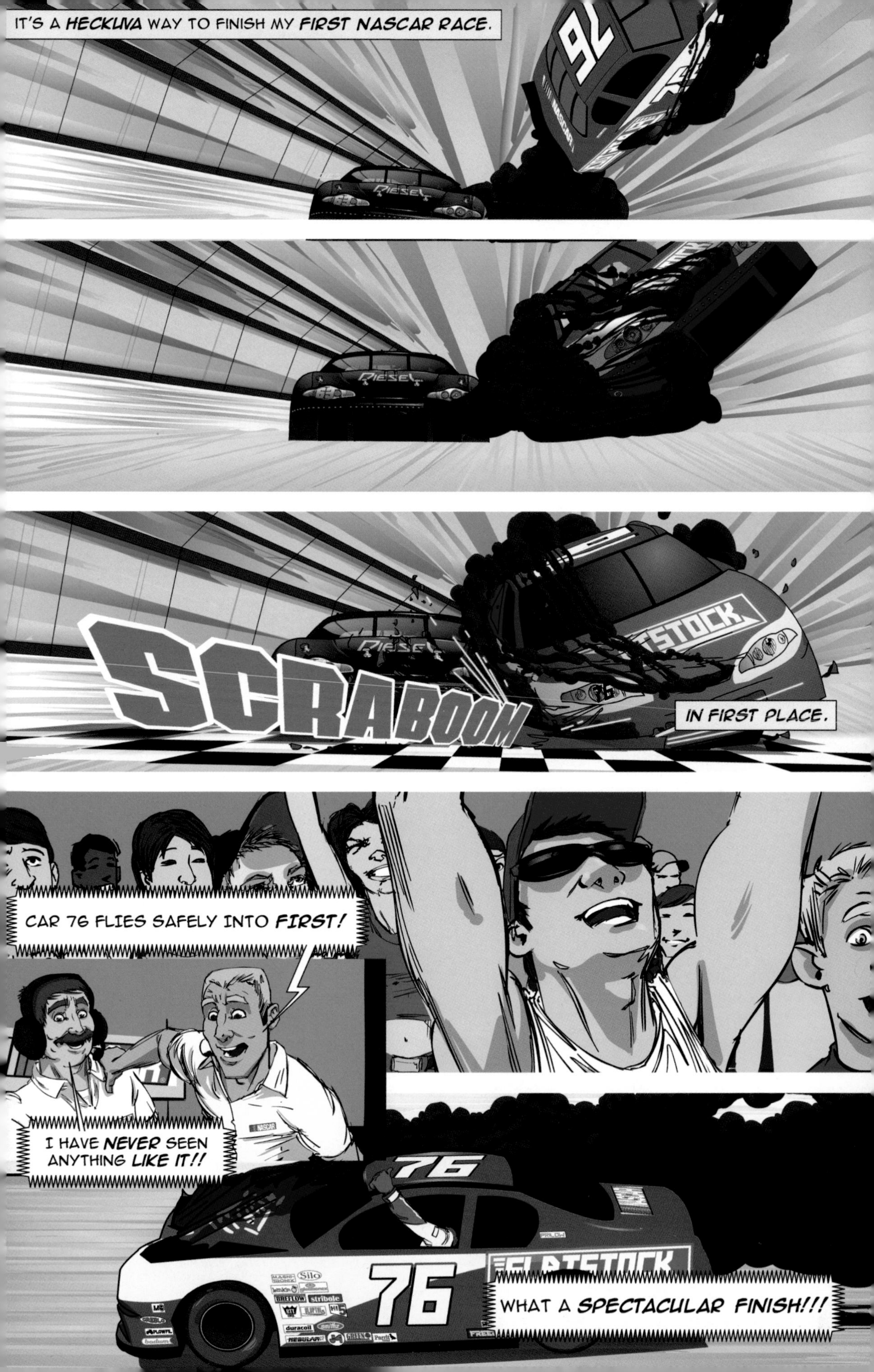
IT'S A HECKUVA WAY TO FINISH MY FIRST NASCAR RACE.
SCRABOOM
IN FIRST PLACE.
CAR 76 FLIES SAFELY INTO FIRST!
I HAVE NEVER SEEN ANYTHING LIKE IT!!
WHAT A SPECTACULAR FINISH!!!

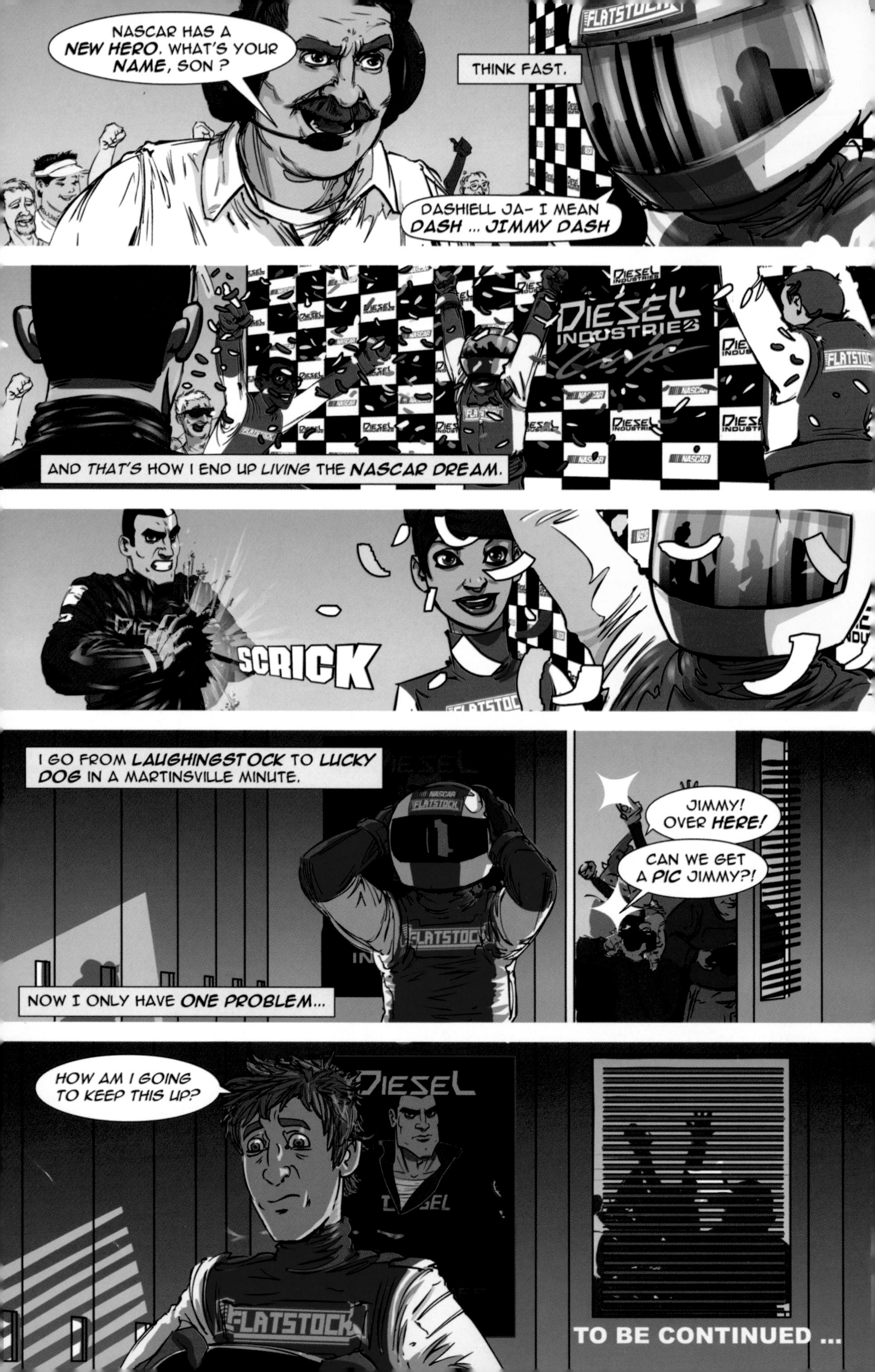

NASCAR HAS A NEW HERO. WHAT'S YOUR NAME, SON ?
THINK FAST.
DASHIELL JA- I MEAN DASH ... JIMMY DASH
AND THAT'S HOW I END UP LIVING THE NASCAR DREAM.
SCRICK
I GO FROM LAUGHINGSTOCK TO LUCKY DOG IN A MARTINSVILLE MINUTE.
NOW I ONLY HAVE ONE PROBLEM...
JIMMY! OVER HERE!
CAN WE GET A PIC JIMMY?!
HOW AM I GOING TO KEEP THIS UP?
TO BE CONTINUED ...

HOW TO DRAW JIMMY DASH

NASCAR COMICS

BY JOHN GALLAGHER

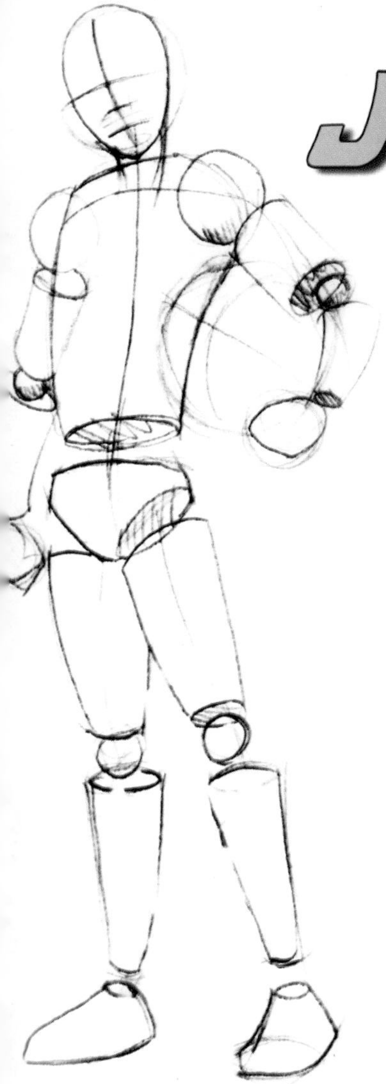

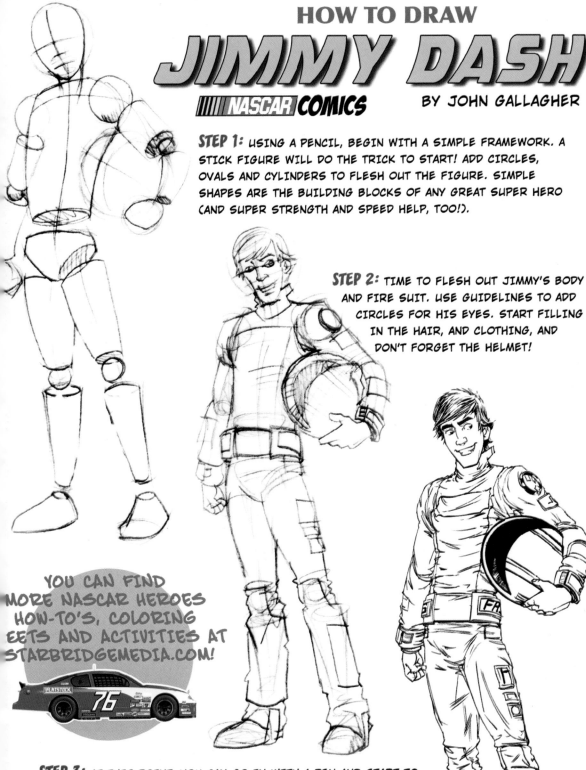

STEP 1: USING A PENCIL, BEGIN WITH A SIMPLE FRAMEWORK. A STICK FIGURE WILL DO THE TRICK TO START! ADD CIRCLES, OVALS AND CYLINDERS TO FLESH OUT THE FIGURE. SIMPLE SHAPES ARE THE BUILDING BLOCKS OF ANY GREAT SUPER HERO (AND SUPER STRENGTH AND SPEED HELP, TOO!).

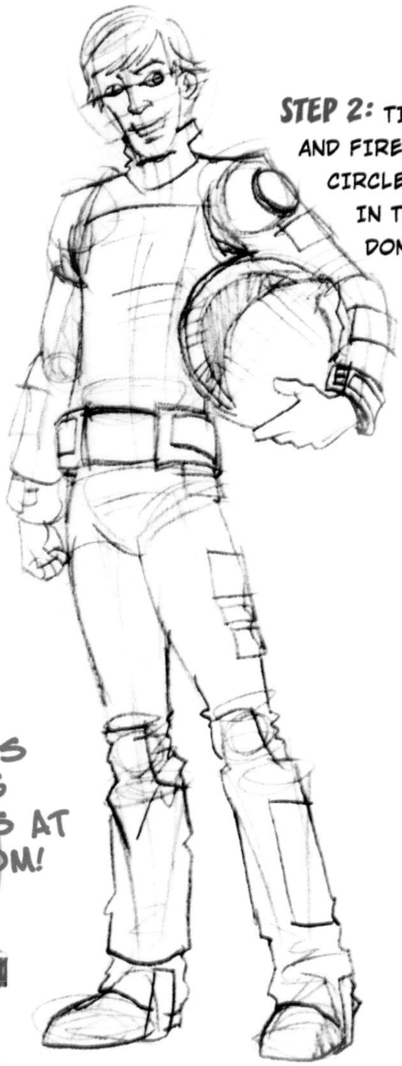

STEP 2: TIME TO FLESH OUT JIMMY'S BODY AND FIRE SUIT. USE GUIDELINES TO ADD CIRCLES FOR HIS EYES. START FILLING IN THE HAIR, AND CLOTHING, AND DON'T FORGET THE HELMET!

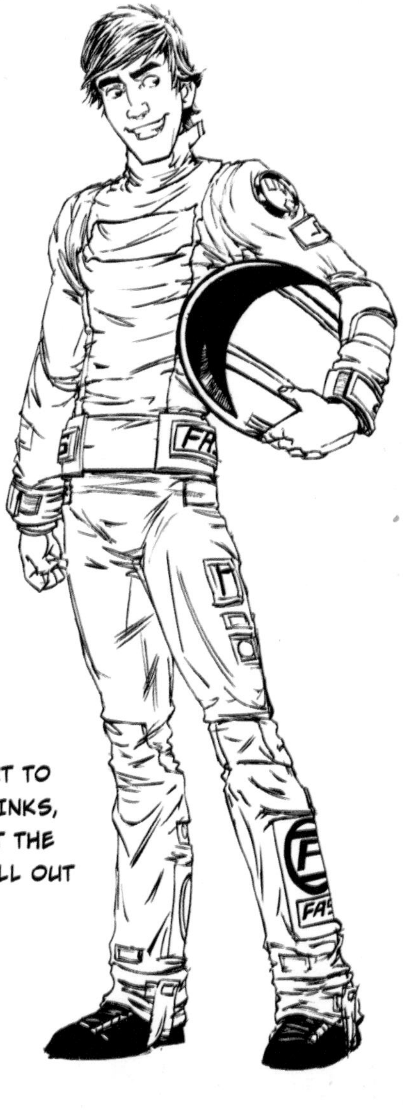
FA
F
FAS

YOU CAN FIND MORE NASCAR HEROES HOW-TO'S, COLORING EETS AND ACTIVITIES AT STARBRIDGEMEDIA.COM!

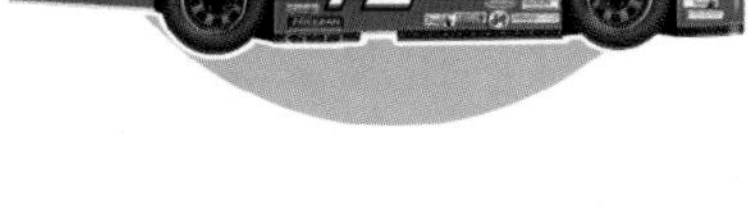
FLATSTOCK
76

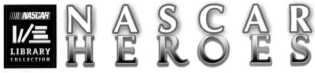

STEP 3: AT THIS POINT, YOU CAN GO IN WITH A PEN AND START TO INK THE FIGURE. ERASE THE PENCIL LINES UNDERNEATH THE INKS, FIXING ANY MISTAKES IN YOUR DRAWINGS. REMEMBER TO LET THE PEN INK DRY BEFORE ERASING, TO AVOID SMUDGES! NOW, PULL OUT YOUR MARKERS OR CRAYONS, AND ADD SOME COLOR!

NASCAR LIBRARY COLLECTION

NASCAR HEROES

HOW TO DRAW NASCAR COMICS

JACK DIESEL'S NO. 63

BY JOHN GALLAGHER

SURE, JACK DIESEL'S A BAD GUY, BUT HE'S GOT A SET OF WHEELS THAT MAKE HIM A NASCAR SUPERSTAR! HERE'S A QUICK GUIDE ON HOW YOU CAN DRAW JACK'S RIDE!

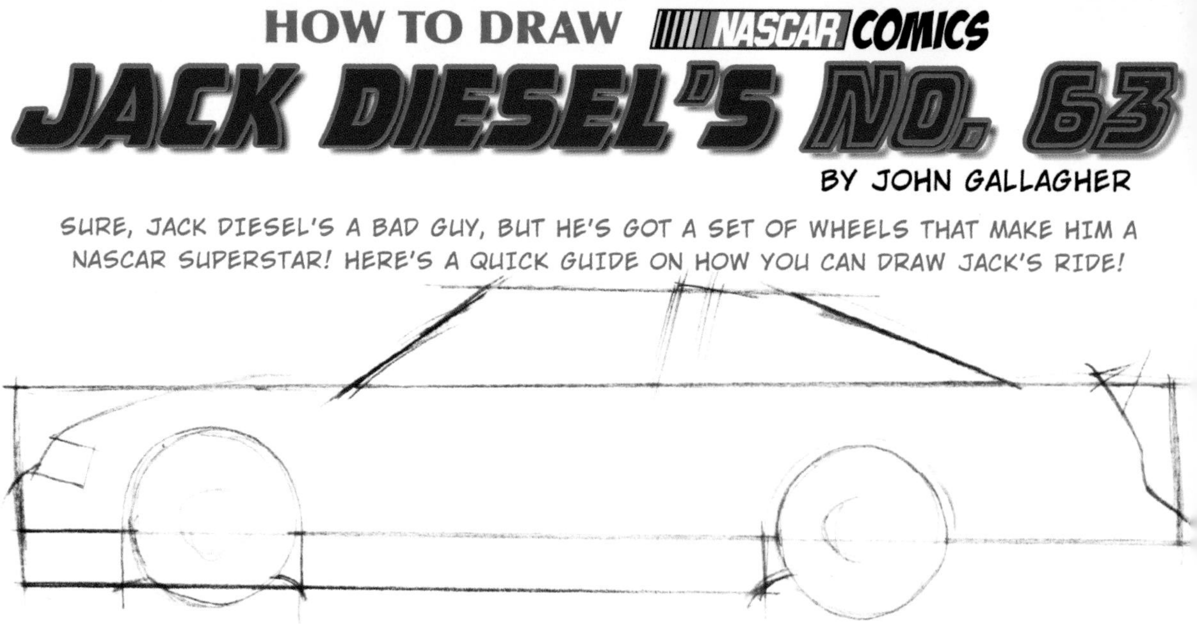

STEP 1: START OFF BY DRAWING A SERIES OF BOXES, SUGGESTING THE SHAPE OF THE CAR AND TIRES. IT'S LIKE CREATING A SHAPE WITH BUILDING BLOCKS, THEN CARVING AWAY AT THE SHAPE INSIDE. YOU CAN DO THIS FREEHAND, OR WITH A RULER, DEPENDING ON HOW "TIGHT" YOU WANT YOUR DRAWING!

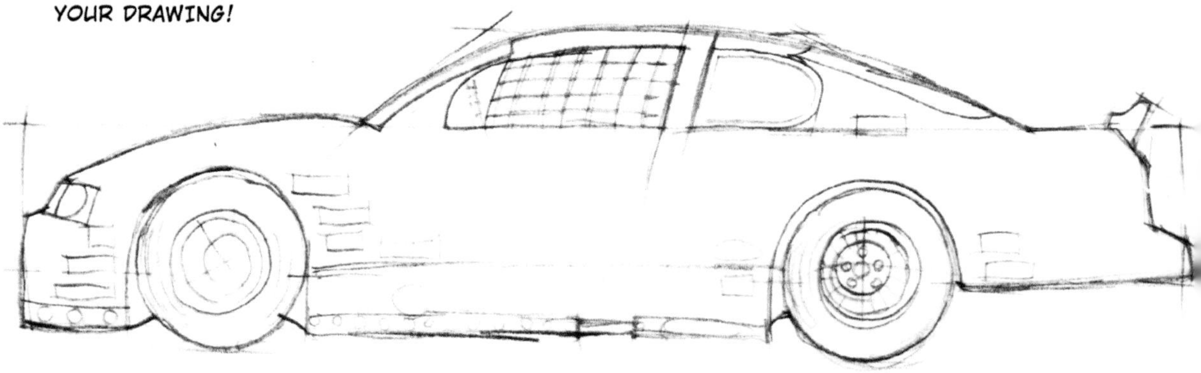

STEP 2: NOW, START TO ZERO IN ON THE SHAPE OF THE CAR FRONT, WINDOWS, TIRES, AND REAR SPOILER. THEN, YOU'LL WANT TO ADD THE DETAILS THAT MAKE A NASCAR UNIQUE, LIKE DECALS, NUMBERS, AND RIVETS!

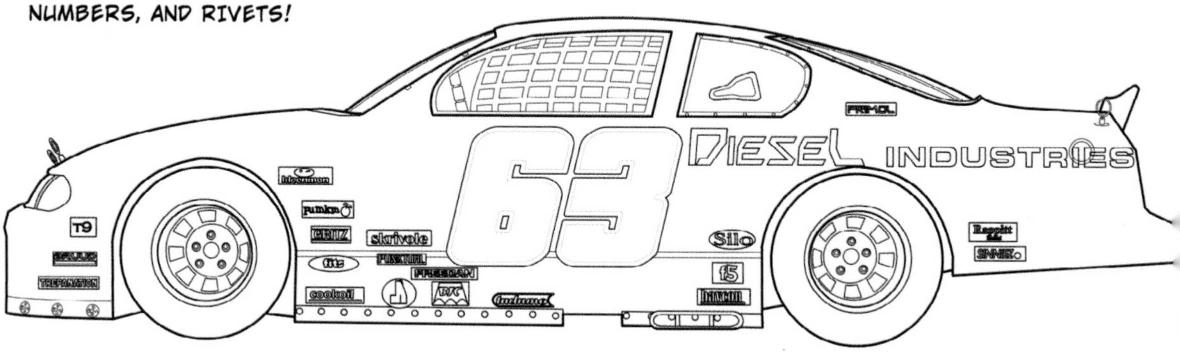
63
DIESEL
INDUSTRIES
T9
skrivole
Silo
f5

STEP 3: AT THIS POINT, YOU CAN GO IN WITH A PEN AND START TO INK THE CAR, REALLY SHARPENING THE IMAGE! ERASE THE PENCIL LINES UNDERNEATH THE INKS, FIXING ANY MISTAKES IN YOUR DRAWING. GIVE THE CAR THE NUMBER OF YOUR FAVORITE DRIVE (BUT DON'T TELL JACK!), AND ADD SOME COLOR! NOW YOUR DRAWING IS READY TO RACE!

NASCAR LIBRARY COLLECTION

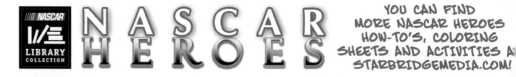

NASCAR HEROES

YOU CAN FIND MORE NASCAR HEROES HOW-TO'S, COLORING SHEETS AND ACTIVITIES A STARBRIDGEMEDIA.COM!